Escape on Monday

Dianne Doubtfire

SCHOLASTIC BOOK SERVICES
New York Toronto London Auckland Sydney Tokyo

Because *Escape on Monday* was first published in England, British spellings have been retained in this American edition.

Cover Design by Dennis Barnett

© Dianne Doubtfire 1970. All rights reserved. Published by Scholastic Book Services, a division of Scholastic Magazines, Inc.

2nd printing .... November 1973
Printed in the U. S. A.

Contents

Dedicated with affection
to Cowes High School

SATURDAY

1

Veronica had hoped to get out of the house without being seen. She tiptoed down the steep narrow stairs, but they always creaked, and she listened breathlessly to the clink of crockery in the kitchen. Her mother was washing up the lunch things.

Veronica was wearing a new red mini-skirt, the shortest she had ever had. She'd bought it that morning for the most important occasion of her life — her first date with Terry Marchmont. She was meeting him at the Regal Cinema in Blackford at two o'clock that afternoon.

If her mother saw her in the new skirt there was bound to be a scene. She was so narrow-minded and unsympathetic that Veronica was forced to be deceitful about quite normal activities. She could never tell her mother anything, it seemed, without getting into trouble. It had always been the same, and now, at sixteen and a half, she was used to it. Nevertheless, there was never a day when her mother didn't make her miserable, and she dreaded the perpetual arguments because they gave her a stomachache. That was what she dreaded now; she couldn't bear the thought of going to meet Terry with a stomachache. . . .

It was now one-fifty. It took ten minutes to walk to the town-centre and she didn't believe in being late on purpose when she went to meet a boy. She reached the hall safely, the gloomy little hall with its old-fashioned wallpaper and dark brown paintwork. Blackford was a dreary north-London suburb and the Masons lived in a small terrace house next to the railway line. There was no garden and the windows rattled every time a train went by. These things wouldn't have mattered if they had been a happy family, but Number 5, Moon Street didn't have the cosy feel of a home. Mrs. Mason wouldn't have an ornament or a cushion out of place, and she was angry if she found a crumb on the floor or a fingermark on the paintwork.

Veronica was just going to open the front door and escape into the April sunshine, when her mother came into the hall from the kitchen. She must have heard the creaking stairs after all.

Ethel Mason was a tall, thin woman with small glittering eyes and sleek black hair. She had always reminded Veronica of a crow, with her neat, dark clothes, her sharp nose, and the way she poked her head forward. Now as she stood in the hall, drying her big red hands on her apron, her brow was creased with the usual worried frown. At first she did not see the new mini-skirt but when she did, the frown deepened into an angry scowl.

"You're not going out in *that*!" she rasped. "So you needn't think you are."

"Why not?" said Veronica. It was not really meant as a question but her mother took it for one and answered it in no uncertain terms.

"Because it's disgusting, that's why not. *Disgusting!* If you could only *see* yourself!"

"I *can* see myself." Veronica glanced into the long mirror beside the coat-pegs. She thought she looked her very best. The new skirt, in glowing crimson corduroy, was stunning, and her thin grey sweater clung smoothly to the small but shapely curves of

7

her breasts. She tossed back her long brown hair, hitched the red sling bag more firmly onto her shoulder, and opened the front door.

Her mother grabbed her roughly by the arm and slammed the door shut. "You're not going out like that," she cried. "Go upstairs and take off that skirt this minute — if you can call it a skirt. Showing all you've got!"

"I'm not showing anything, Mother. I've got tights on — look!" She lifted the skirt to reveal sheer nylon tights and black briefs. Her legs were long and perfect; mini-skirts were made for girls like Veronica.

"I said go and take it off this *minute*."

"But I only bought it this morning." Veronica could not keep the tremor from her voice. "I've been saving up for weeks."

"I can't help that. Hurry up — I'm waiting."

Veronica clenched her teeth. She'd have to put on her old black mini-skirt which was four inches longer than the new one and not half so fetching. She'd have to get moving, too, or she'd be late to meet Terry, even if she ran all the way.

She was just turning towards the staircase when her mother spoke again: "Put that brown check skirt on," she said.

If she had told Veronica to cut off all her hair she could hardly have made her more angry or miserable. The brown check could not really be called a mini-skirt at all; Veronica had long ago stuffed it into the back of a drawer.

"I — I can't," she stuttered. "I've put it away to give to a jumble sale — it's *ancient*."

"How dare you give away your clothes without my permission. Who buys your clothes for you, tell me that?"

"Daddy does. And he'd *never* tell me to wear that ghastly old horror. He ——"

"You leave your father out of this. He hasn't the guts to tell you to do anything."

Veronica's eyes began to ache with tears. For as long as she could remember, her mother had criticised her appearance and found fault with everything she did. She had no idea why this should be, and when she was small she had simply been frightened and unhappy about it. But as she grew older, her fear and misery had gradually intensified into anger and resentment. Now she had to admit to herself that she positively hated her mother. She hated her for her constant unkindness and lack of understanding, but most of all for the way she treated her father.

George Mason was a mild little man with a long bony face and sad brown eyes. He worked in a furniture shop in Blackford, but after thirty years with the same firm he was still a salesman and Mrs. Mason was always reminding him of it.

He spent every spare moment in a tiny shed in the backyard — his workshop, he called it — making exquisite little models of old sailing ships. Veronica knew that he went there to escape; it was the same reason that drove her to the Youth Club or the Discotheque every night. She would have liked to spend cosy evenings at home, reading or watching television or entertaining her friends, but there was no pleasure in being in the same house with her mother. If she wasn't snapping your head off she was polishing the floor under your feet.

Now Veronica looked at her watch to hide the tears that were misting her eyes. It was already two o'clock.

"I'll have to go, Mum," said Veronica. "Or I'll be late."

Terry would be there by now, waiting for her at the Regal — Terry, the one boy in the world she had dreamed of going out with, Terry with his long fair hair and warm, attentive brown eyes. He was a motor mechanic by trade but he was also a poet. He wrote beautiful, melancholy lyrics for folk songs and sang them in a soft, low voice that turned Veronica's heart over.

She had often been with him in a crowd at the Youth Club but he had always paired off with Jackie Drake. Now at last he had invited Veronica to the pictures — just her, on her own — and she felt it was the most stupendous day of her life. She *had* to wear the new red skirt; she had to look special to compete with Jackie.

Her mother was glaring at her in silence. "I'll *have* to go now, Mum," she repeated.

"You will not leave this house in that skirt."

Veronica drew a deep breath. "But I'm supposed to be meeting Dolly at two. We'll miss the start of the picture. Please, Mum!" She couldn't tell her mother about Terry because she had forbidden her to go out with boys. Dolly Frost had been at Blackford Secondary School with her a good natured fat girl with a round babyish face, who moaned incessantly about her size but was forever eating cream buns and chocolate. Mrs. Mason approved of her because she had brought her a bunch of yellow tulips when she came to tea the previous week. Besides, Dolly wore longish skirts; she had to because her legs were like huge pink balloons.

Now Mrs. Mason looked at Veronica keenly. "Where are you meeting Dolly, then?"

"Outside the Regal."

Mrs. Mason hesitated for a moment, still

watching her daughter's face, then she took off her apron and reached up for her green tweed coat which was hanging beside the mirror. "I'll come along with you," she said. "I've got to collect your father's trousers from the cleaner's."

Veronica felt her cheeks go hot but before she could think of anything to say her mother had pushed the apron into her hands. "Put this in the kitchen," she said, "and then go upstairs and change into that brown check skirt like I told you."

Mrs. Mason began to put on her black felt hat in front of the hall mirror and Veronica, half stupefied, went into the kitchen and threw the apron onto the table. The back door led out of the kitchen through a small yard onto a rough path that ran alongside the railway track. She could see her father at work in his shed, bending over a model galleon, his greying hair gleaming under the electric light. Her stomach was aching again as she stood there, wondering what to do, and as she hesitated a train went rattling by.

Suddenly she made her decision. Under cover of the noise, she slipped out of the back door and fled across the yard. Her father looked up and smiled through the little cobwebby window as she passed, and she waved and blew him a kiss. Then she opened the rickety back gate and went racing down the path towards the town.

She ran as fast as she could, her hair flying, her shoulderbag bumping against her side. Her heart was pounding as she turned into the street that led to the Regal. She hardly dared to imagine her mother's reactions, but for the moment she could only think of Terry. She was actually on her way to meet him; she would be late but no one could stop her now.

2

It was nearly a quarter past two when Veronica came in sight of the Regal, but nevertheless she slowed down to a leisurely walking pace, smoothed her windblown hair and tried to breathe slowly and deeply. She had to play it cool; it would never do for Terry to guess how she felt about him.

The cinema was in the High Street, between Woolworths and the Post Office. The film was an X Certificate called *Brothers in Love*. She hoped it wouldn't be too embarrassingly sexy for her first date with Terry. The title sounded as if it might be about incest or queers — or both — but Jerry had said it ought to be good and she knew he liked the same kind of films as she did. Veronica was rather shy about sex. Her mother had always switched off the television with snorts of disgust if there was anything the least bit outspoken, and she would never let Veronica watch plays; she said they were "full of filth." Her father got nervy at the mere mention of anything sexy and went pink at the sides of his jaws. She had accumulated most of her knowledge about the facts of life from jokes, and from Dolly Frost who had a married sister.

Veronica had never been really keen on a boy before she met Terry. She'd done a bit of petting at parties and in the pictures, but she hadn't really enjoyed it. Sometimes she used to wonder if she was normal, especially as she had a violent passion for the headmistress when she was at Blackford Secondary Modern. When she left school the previous July she'd wept in her bedroom for a whole afternoon at the thought of not seeing her again, and for weeks she kept a snapshot of her stuck to her dressing-table mirror with Sellotape.

In October, when she was sixteen, Veronica started work as an apprentice hairdresser at a salon called Irene's and it was then, with a little money of her own, that she joined the Youth Club. She wasn't keen on the idea at first because she was shy of meeting people, but Dolly Frost talked her into it.

"Ringo's is a super Club," she said. "You can play table tennis and cards and chess and things, and there are more fellows than girls. There's dancing some nights and a smashing snack bar with sausage rolls and jam doughnuts and. . . ." Dolly had got on to her favourite subject — food — and Veronica had stopped listening. But she joined the Club and that was the end of her schoolgirl crushes. It was, in fact, the beginning of her first serious love affair.

She saw Terry Marchmont the first night she went to Ringo's, and there was something about his small face with its helmet of pale hair that haunted her from the first moment. He was not exceptionally good-looking, but there was an appealing serenity about his features, and his large brown eyes seemed to caress everything and everyone they looked at. When he sat cross-legged on the floor and sang his mournful poetic songs without any accompaniment, Veronica was merely one of a dozen other admirers — Jackie Drake included — who crowded round him and implored him to carry on singing.

A few weeks later, Jackie Drake brought a guitar to the Club. She could play it well enough to strum an accompaniment and from that day she became Terry's special friend. Veronica had never seen them together in the town, except in a gang, and she hadn't seen them kissing or even holding hands, but Jackie was very beautiful — small and shapely with curly black hair and an exquisite mouth which she enhanced with shiny pink lipstick. She was nineteen, the same age as Terry, and she made Veronica feel childish and un-sophisticated.

Every day Veronica's love for Terry grew more intense. If he smiled at her she was un-believably happy; if he seemed offhand she was miserable. She thought about him all day at the hairdresser's as she passed rollers and pins to the seniors, swept the floor, or took the clients' coats and showed them to their places. It seemed there would never be any peace or happiness for her without him.

The months went by — January, February, March. He was friendly enough; he offered her cigarettes and chewing gum from time to time, and talked to her about his garage job and the sports car he hoped to buy one day. Once he had even told her she had "smashing legs." But he never asked her out and they only met at Ringo's or when he hap-pened to be in the same group at a snack bar. She'd have seen more of him if she'd been old enough to go into the Spotted Dog;

she knew he often went in there for a beer with his mates from the garage, and sometimes a gang from the Club would vanish through those mysterious doors, Jackie included. It was Jackie who told Veronica that Terry had no father and that his mother ran a boarding house. She seemed to know everything about him.

Then, one evening in April the miracle happened. Veronica had just left Ringo's by herself because her mother had told her to come home early to do some ironing. She was walking slowly up the cobbled side street where the Club was, and noticing with a kind of sad pleasure that some of the buds on the trees were bursting out into little green rosettes, when she heard footsteps running behind her, and a familiar low voice, "Hi, Ronny — hang on a sec!"

She turned and there was Terry, smiling and bright-eyed. A few minutes earlier he'd been singing one of his new songs at the Club; he must have actually noticed her leaving. . . .

"You're off early," he said.

"Yeah — I've got some jobs to do for my mother."

He nodded. "How about coming to the Regal on Saturday?" Unbelievably, he was blushing. "Just you and me," he went on. "Seems like a good picture — it's won an award. Venice Film Festival or something."

Her heart seemed to explode with joy but all she said was "Why not," the cool comment that wasn't even a question.

"Okay, then — two o'clock. We can have a snack at the Club afterwards if you like."

"Yeah. Thanks."

"See you, then." And he was gone, swinging away across the road, a tall slight figure in his tight jeans and tattered, bright-blue anorak.

It had only been a short exchange of simple words, but for Veronica it was the purest poetry. And he had blushed. He had definitely blushed. . . . She raced home, swinging her bag in joyous circles, and not even her mother's sour expression or the mountain of ironing could spoil her happiness.

And now the time had arrived; only she was a quarter of an hour late and her stomach was upset.

She saw Terry through the Saturday shopping crowd before she reached the cinema. He was leaning against the wall by the entrance, his hair blowing across his face, a torn poster flapping in the wind behind his head. He was wearing a white polo-necked sweater and she was overwhelmed with rapture at the thought of going into the cinema and sitting beside him in the secret gloom, their arms touching, perhaps holding hands, perhaps. . . .

Her heart suddenly seemed to jerk inside her as she drew nearer. He was not alone; he was talking to someone. She couldn't see who it was at first, but as she pressed through the crowd and hurried up to him, her heart gave another sickening lurch. Standing in front of him, with her arms folded and her black hair combed into a fancy new style, was Jackie Drake. She was wearing a bright green trouser-suit and as Veronica approached she turned and smiled, her glossy pink lipstick sparkling in the sun.

"I just came by a few minutes ago and Terry was all on his own so I thought I'd keep him company," she said brightly. "Don't let me butt in, though."

Veronica tried to smile but her lips were quivering. "Oh — that's all right —" Then she muttered, "Sorry I'm late, Terry," and prayed he wouldn't notice how upset she was.

He grinned, enclosing them both in his warm brown gaze. "Let's all go in and see what these lecherous *Brothers in Love* are up to," he said. "Come on, girls. We'll go in the Circle and throw fag ends down on the plebs!" He took them both by the arm and bore them into the foyer. Jackie was laughing gaily, making no protest about joining them, and Veronica's stomach was aching more than ever.

There was nothing to be done. Terry was buying three tickets instead of two; the longed-for date was in ruins before it had even begun. And it was all her mother's fault.

3

The big picture had started when they arrived in the Circle. "Front row!" whispered Terry as they filed down the aisle in the flickering light from the screen.

Jackie led the way, with Terry behind them both, and Veronica felt a wave of relief as she realised that she would be sitting in the middle; Jackie wouldn't be next to Terry. There were plenty of vacant seats and the usherette flashed her torch along the front row. At this moment, however, Jackie stepped back and gently pushed Veronica ahead of her, so that Veronica found herself sitting between Jackie and an old man. There was nothing she could do but sit there calmly and pretend she didn't mind, but she felt so angry and disappointed that she could have cried.

She glanced at Terry, on the other side of Jackie, and saw him settling himself in his seat, trying to accommodate his long legs in the narrow space. Jackie was snuggling down comfortably, leaning sideways with her elbow on the armrest next to Terry. She always seemed so composed, so perfectly at ease.

Veronica never really knew what the film was about. She stared at the picture without taking it in, aware of nothing but Terry's profile in the half light, and the movements of his hand as he drew on a cigarette and flicked the ash away from time to time. Jackie was chewing, her jaws moving steadily; apart from that she was perfectly still and Veronica felt sure that her shoulder was pressed against Terry's arm. Terry, however, seemed to be engrossed in the film, and she consoled herself with the thought that perhaps he himself was disappointed about the seating arrangements. Veronica was appalled that Jackie could have behaved so meanly after crashing in on their date.

When the lights went up for the interval Veronica crossed her legs and smoothed her new mini-skirt but Terry was busy talking to Jackie about the next film, a documentary about whaling, and she felt so moody and tense that she could not resist interrupting them to ask Terry for a cigarette, although she really hated smoking. When she leaned across for a light he smiled at her over the flame of the match and she was sure she detected a faint conspiratorial wink.

He said to them both, "How about tea at Mamie's after this?" Mamie's was an Old World Tea Room with a low, timbered ceiling and latticed windows. It was renowned for its huge toasted tea cakes running with butter, and homemade raspberry tarts.

"That would be super," said Veronica, blowing smoke down her nostrils in an effort to appear calm and self-assured.

"I can't — sorry," said Jackie, still chewing. "I've a guitar lesson at half-past five."

Veronica's heart leapt with delight. Tea at Mamie's — alone with Terry at last! Perhaps, after all, the day could be redeemed.

When the programme was over, Jackie said she must dash off or she'd be late for her lesson, and Terry and Veronica went slowly down the steps with the crowd towards the exit. As they crossed the foyer he put his arm round her shoulders.

"Sorry it worked out like that," he said. "There wasn't much I could do about it."

"That's all right," she said, but it was much more than all right. Suddenly she felt pretty and graceful again; her body seemed as light as air, and she looked up at him with a bright, easy smile as they went out through the swing doors.

"Thanks for taking me," she said. "Smashing seats — I'd never been in the Circle before."

His arm was still round her shoulder and she felt his hand on her hair, stroking it affectionately.

"Some girls would've kept that dark," he said. "They'd have made out they always went in the Circle."

They were out in the street with the wind lifting their hair and Terry stopped to look at her, taking her hand and smiling down at her. She was happily conscious of her new skirt and long graceful legs.

"You look great," he said. "That mini's a knockout."

She laughed with pleasure. "My mother doesn't think so. She told me I hadn't to wear it. I had to nip out the back way — that's why I was late."

"A bit old-fashioned, is she, then?"

"She's worse than old-fashioned. She does everything she can to make me miserable," said Veronica. "She always has."

"You poor chick! What's wrong with her, then?"

"What's right with her!"

"No, but I mean, is she sick or something?"

At that moment Veronica let out a gasp of horror. "She's *there*! She's just over there. I think she's seen me ——" She clung to Terry's hand and tried to hide behind him but her mother was pushing through the crowd towards them, a tall menacing figure in her long coat and felt hat. Her face was distorted with rage, and she seized Veronica by the arm and pulled her viciously away from Terry.

"You liar!" she cried. "You wicked, deceitful little liar! You told me you were meeting Dolly Frost, didn't you?"

Veronica looked at her mother in silence; she couldn't bear the thought of a scene in front of Terry.

"*Didn't you?*"

She nodded. "It was only because ——"

Mrs. Mason did not wait for a reply. She was staring with contempt at Terry's long hair, grubby sweater, and tight jeans. "As for you," she snarled at him, "if I ever see you with my daughter again you'll be sorry for it. When she's old enough to go to the cinema with a boy he won't be a long-haired thug of *your* kind, I can tell you that! He'll be a decent, clean-living boy with a pride in his appearance. And you ought to be ashamed — taking a girl to see that kind of filthy rubbish ——" She indicated the Regal poster.

"It was a super film!" cried Veronica.

"Be quiet!" shouted her mother.

"Veronica's right," said Terry quietly. "It's a very fine film. It won an award at the Venice Festival. And she isn't under age or anything——"

"How *dare* you argue with me! Get out of my sight — and if I ever see Veronica with you again, you'll both wish you'd never been born!"

Veronica saw Terry's face turn crimson and then white. For a moment he stood quite still, looking at Mrs. Mason with mingled fury and astonishment. Then he turned to Veronica and put his hand gently on her shoulder. "Sorry, Ronny," he said. "Take it easy, kid."

He walked swiftly away through the crowd, and Mrs. Mason turned on her daughter, her small eyes dark with rage.

"You'll stay in your room till tomorrow," she said. "Locked in, with nothing to eat. And another thing — you aren't going to that Club place anymore, do you hear?"

Veronica burst into tears and let out a storm of angry protest, but she was forced to accompany her mother back to the house.

4

For more than an hour Veronica lay face down on her bed, overcome with anguish. She cried until her eyes were swollen and sore and her nose was so congested that she could only breathe through her mouth. She was desperately thirsty but when she hammered on the door and called to her mother for a glass of water, there was no reply.

She could hear music from the television in the sitting room. Her mother would be looking in, as usual, with Mrs. Wainwright, a hunched-up little woman with horn-rimmed spectacles and no neck, who lived opposite. Mrs. Wainwright would be on her mother's side about Veronica; she was the same kind of person — the kind who was disgusted by mini-skirts and thought every boy with long hair was a hooligan.

Veronica wanted desperately to talk to her father. He had been out when they returned and he probably wouldn't be back until suppertime at half-past seven. He often went for a walk in the park on Saturday afternoons, but her mother would never go with him. She hated the park, she said, though Veronica thought it a beautiful place, with its vast lawns and towering trees. Sometimes she went there with her father. They never said very much, just watched the people and enjoyed walking on the grass; there was nowhere else in Blackford where you could walk on grass. He occasionally talked about his wartime adventures in the Navy, or Veronica would tell him about her work at Irene's and the fun they had at the Club, but what she really wanted was to talk to him about her mother. She longed to pour out her misery and ask for his help, but every time she tried, he became distant and withdrawn; it was as if he was closing a door in her face. She supposed he felt it would be disloyal to allow her to complain, but she knew that he understood a great deal of what she went through because he suffered in the same way himself.

She got up and went to the bedroom window, praying to see him come in through the back gate. The time had surely come for her to *force* him to listen. She would make him understand that she was in love with Terry and that she couldn't possibly stop going to the Club. Her father must be made to realise just how cruel her mother was, and he must be persuaded to do something about it. He was far too docile, that was the trouble. He always seemed to do whatever her mother suggested, without any argument.

Veronica looked down into the little concrete yard. There was a brick wall all round it and her father's workshed was built against the wall in the corner by the gate. Apart from the shed there was nothing in the yard but a dustbin; there was hardly room for anything else.

It was getting dark; the houses at the other side of the railway line were like grey cutouts against the evening sky. A faint star sparkled between the masts of a television aerial and a few of the windows were already showing lights. Saturday night! She would have had tea at Mamie's with Terry and then gone on to Ringo's with him. He might even have taken her to the Discotheque. . . .

The tears came welling into her eyes again and she leaned her forehead against the cold glass. If only she could climb out and escape! She pushed up the window and leaned out. It was much too high to jump, and there was nothing to hold on to, nothing but a sheer brick wall with the kitchen window a long way below. She thought of joining two sheets together like people in burning houses did, but she was scared of heights, and in any case she wasn't the tomboyish kind of girl who could manage such an escapade.

She sat down on the bed with the idea of listening to some pop music on her transistor, but when she turned to the bedside table to switch it on, she found it had gone. Her mother must have taken it away. She sighed with irritation. All right, she'd carry on reading a paperback book that Dolly Frost had lent her. It was supposed to be wickedly sexy but Veronica was finding it quite boring. Still, it would pass the time.

It was now too dark to read so she went to the door to switch on the light. Nothing happened; the switch wasn't working. Puzzled, she looked up under the fringed yellow shade and saw to her horror that there was no electric light bulb in the socket. So her mother had taken that as well! She must have prepared the room as a punishment chamber while Veronica was at the pictures.

She stood in the middle of the room, her

pulses throbbing with hatred. She felt she could easily have picked up the bedside table in her fury and hurled it across the room. She pressed her fist against her mouth, biting the knuckles until she almost drew blood. What had she done to deserve a mother like that? What had she *done*?

She ran to the window and looked down into the yard, gripped by a fearful urge to throw herself to destruction. She stared down wildly, imagining her body lying on the concrete, broken and bleeding. Perhaps her mother would be sorry when it was too late. . . .

"Hello, Veronica!" Her father was standing at the back gate, a slight, shadowy figure in the dusk.

Her heart leapt with thankfulness. "Daddy — oh, Daddy!"

He came into the yard and stood looking up at her, his thin hair ruffled by the wind. "What's the matter, pet? You look as if you'd seen a ghost."

"She's locked me in," cried Veronica in a frenzied whisper. "Come and let me out — please, Daddy — I shall *die* if you don't let me out!"

He hesitated, pulling at his tie as he often did when he was worried, but she could not endure his hesitation. She wanted him to help her instantly, without having to think about it.

"Daddy — *please*!"

"What have you done, Veronica?" His voice was low and despairing.

"Nothing. Nothing wrong — I *promise* ——"

"All right. Hang on, and I'll see."

"The key's in the lock," she said. "I can see it from this side. And she's taken the bulb out of the light — I can't read or ——"

But he was gone. She heard him open the kitchen door and close it again very quietly.

She shut the window and turned back into the room. It was now so dark that she could only see the shiny things — her dressing-table mirror reflecting the evening sky, a glass jar of talcum powder, the silver buckle of a belt hanging over the bedrail. She could also see under the bed the white glint of the chamber pot her mother had brought in to save unlocking the door for Veronica to go to the lavatory. She peered at herself in the mirror but she could only see the dim blur of her face and the glimmer of a tear still wet on her cheek.

After a while she heard the stairs creaking, followed by footsteps on the landing. Then the key grated in the lock and the brass doorknob caught the light from the window as it slowly began to turn.

5

Mr. Mason came into Veronica's room and shut the door silently behind him. She rushed into his arms and clung to him as if she would never let him go.

"Your mother'll murder me if she finds out," he whispered.

"Where is she?"

"In the sitting room with Mrs. Wainwright. They're talking fifteen to the dozen about the Church Bazaar so it should be all right for a while."

"I'll lock us in," said Veronica, and in spite of her father's vague protest she went to the door and changed the key to the inside, turning it in the lock.

He sat down on the bed. "I couldn't bring the light bulb," he said. "I don't know where she's put it and I haven't got another one. Besides——"

"Never mind." Veronica squatted on the floor at his feet and looked up at him. She could just make out the bony outline of his cheek and nose, and the gleam of his sad eyes. His white collar caught the last of the light.

She drew a deep breath. "Daddy — you've got to listen to me — you've got to let me talk to you — about *her*. You've never let me say anything before — but you've *got* to!"

He nodded his head. "I know," he said, and his voice was trembling.

"I can't bear it any longer," she said. "She's so *horrible* to me — she does everything she can to make me miserable."

"I know," he said again.

"Why is it?" she said. "Why? What have I *done*?"

"It's not your fault. It's something she can't help. She's unhappy, that's the trouble. Terribly unhappy. She feels she's never had the things she wanted out of life."

"What did she want?" said Veronica.

"Oh, all the usual things — a fine house, servants, beautiful clothes. I've been a failure, you see, from her point of view. Besides——"

"But lots of people live like us — without much money — and they're perfectly happy."

"Yes, but—— " He hesitated.

"But what?"

"She wanted a son — you know that, don't you? She really wanted a boy when you were born. And of course she's never got over losing Nigel." Nigel was Veronica's brother who had died when he was ten months old. Veronica was three when it happened and she didn't remember him.

"But that was *ages* ago!"

"Yes, but people can't forget things when they're unhappy. She hates living here — hates this place with the railway line and the dirt and everything ——"

"She hates *me*, I know that much," cried Veronica.

"Ssssh!" He gently touched her shoulder, and she was reminded of the way Terry had touched her that afternoon just before he left her. She wondered what he was doing now and if Jackie was with him. . . .

Her father was silent for a while and then he said, "I think your mother hates everybody and everything. I don't know what we can do about it — I wish to God I did. Tell me what happened this afternoon. I know you went out in a very short skirt after she told you to change ——"

"It's a beautiful skirt, Daddy." She looked down at it in the gloom and felt the soft corduroy, warm against the curve of her hip. "I bought it specially — it was fifty-nine and six."

"I'm sure it's lovely, but you've got to remember that your mother has funny ideas about young people. She can't get used to the way you all dress these days."

"It isn't only that," said Veronica. She felt the tears coming into her eyes as she thought about Terry but she forced them back. She couldn't explain things properly if she was crying.

"Tell me everything," said her father. "Right from the beginning. Just tell me everything that's worrying you."

When she had finished it was quite dark; she couldn't even see her father's white collar. She told him about her love for Terry, her jealousy of Jackie Drake, her hopelessness until that week when he had invited her to the Regal. She confessed to the lie about meeting Dolly Frost and she told him exactly what her mother had said to Terry outside the cinema.

"And I'm going to go on seeing him whatever *anybody* says," she said finally. "Not even you can stop me, Daddy."

"I wouldn't want to stop you, pet. You're old enough now to have a boyfriend — though you'll probably change your mind a few times yet —"

Veronica shook her head vehemently. "No, I shan't. I shall always love Terry," she said solemnly. "Always. If I can't have him, I don't want anybody."

"I know how you feel," said her father, and he reached out in the darkness to comfort her. She clung to his hand and pressed it against her cheek. She knew that he understood and she worshipped him for it.

He got up and went to the window. The floorboards creaked and she was afraid her mother might come.

"What am I going to *do*?" she asked him. "What am I going to do about seeing Terry and going to the Club and everything?"

There was a long silence and she was relieved to hear the chattering voices of her mother and Mrs. Wainwright coming faintly from the sitting room.

At last her father drew a deep breath. "I want you to tell me something, Veronica."

"What?" His tone of voice frightened her a little.

"You're not thinking of — of sleeping with this boy, are you?"

Veronica found this difficult to answer; she didn't really know how she would feel about it if the question arose. "I shouldn't think so," she said. "Why? Does it matter?"

"Veronica! You *know* it matters."

"Not if we loved each other."

"Yes — even then. You're too young to get married for a long time yet."

"Who said anything about getting married?"

"I know, I know. I suppose I'm old-fashioned but I hate the thought of you — sleeping with a boy — and then changing your mind about him."

She wondered what he would think if he heard some of the conversations at the Club. "But I've *told* you, Daddy — I shan't change my mind."

"You can say that now, but how can you be sure? You must have seen it happen with your friends. And then someone else comes along and you think *that'll* be forever. But it isn't, and so it goes on. And if you're — going the whole hog — it's — oh, I don't know ——" He sighed. "I know it's different nowadays, but I just want you to be happy, pet. You know that's all I want."

"You don't have to worry, Daddy. I'd never be daft enough to get a baby or anything. Honest."

"And you wouldn't feel you wanted to — to save yourself for the man you marry?"

"I don't reckon much about marriage," she said. "I mean, look at you and Mother! It's loving each other that counts — not gabbling a few words in church. Loving each other and being kind to each other."

A train went by and she could see her father's profile in the light from the carriages.

He looked so sad and concerned that her heart suddenly ached for him. She understood, as never before, how much he loved her and how kind he was to risk a terrible scene with her mother by coming up to her bedroom like this. It must be an effort, too, to talk to her about sex when he found it so embarrassing. She guessed he would never have been able to do it if it hadn't been for the darkness.

He was silent for a while after the train had passed. Then he said, "That may be all right so long as there aren't children to consider ——"

Veronica gave a bitter little laugh. "I'd jolly well rather have a mother that *wasn't* married if she *loved* me," she said, "rather than the one I've got!"

"Oh, Veronica!" His voice was almost a sob and she wished she could take it back, even though it was true.

"It's not *your* fault," she said, trying to make amends. "You couldn't have known what she was like, or you'd never have married her, would you?"

"She was different then," he said. He broke off as the front door banged downstairs, and Veronica realised with a throb of fright that it probably meant that Mrs. Wainwright had gone.

"Quick, Daddy ——" she whispered. "Go out and lock me in again. Pretend you've been in the bathroom. *Quick!*"

She got up and rushed to the door, stumbling in the darkness. In a moment she had opened it and thrust the key into his hand. "Thank you — *darling* Daddy. Thank you for coming!" She pushed him out and he closed the door, locking it behind him. A few moments later she heard him in the bathroom and she knew that he was safe.

She leaned against the door, and although her knees were trembling she felt a strange release from the anguish she had felt before. She had been able to talk to him at last — and he was on her side. Thank God, he was on her side.

After a while she heard the toilet flush and then her mother's voice came echoing up the stairs.

"George! I didn't know you were back — where on earth have you been? I want my supper and you haven't even put the kettle on. *George!*"

"Coming, dear."

Veronica groaned with irritation. Why did he let her boss him about like that? Why had he let her get away with it for all those years? It was so weak and so dishonest — "*Coming, dear. . . .*" What must he really be

41

thinking? If he'd told her what he really thought, right from the start, she might never have got like that. And yet. . . . Veronica knew from her own experience how hopeless it was to fight against her mother's persistent nagging. It only made things worse. And in any case, her father simply wasn't the fighting kind.

She lay on the bed in the darkness and thought about Terry. Of course, he wasn't the fighting kind either. The songs he wrote were a proof of that, if you needed any proof. Maybe that was the way one ought to be — serene and unresisting. But surely you had to put your foot down *somewhere*. Hadn't you?

Whatever happened, she was determined to go to the Club the next day. It didn't open till half-past two on Sundays but she'd be here. And what was more, she'd jolly well wear her new mini-skirt.

SUNDAY

6

That night Veronica had a peculiar dream. For the first time in her life, as far as she could remember, she dreamed about her baby brother, Nigel. Her parents never spoke of him, and his death had always been a kind of unmentionable horror. She had asked her grandmother about him when she was about ten and had been told "never to talk about him again," as if she had committed some terrible crime by mentioning his name. She understood, of course, what a tragedy it must have been for her parents to lose him when he was nearly a year old, but she would have liked to talk about him openly, instead of feeling uncomfortable about it.

She had seen a tinted photograph of him,

solemn and wide-eyed with fat cheeks and a
tuft of hair combed carefully into a big
shiny curl. His mother must have combed it
like that for the photograph. His mother! It
was odd to think that Nigel's mother was also
her mother, and that she had loved this baby.
Perhaps she had even loved Veronica as a
baby. . . . Or had she always hated her, just
for being a girl?

In the dream, Veronica was pushing Nigel
in his pram through a wood, and cascades of
red petals kept falling from the trees, filling
the pram and making a crimson carpet on the
ground. The colour of the petals was so clear
in her dream that Veronica's first thought on
waking was: "I dreamed in colour!" A boy
at Ringo's called Jeremy Wright had said that
you couldn't dream in colour and nobody
had contradicted him. She looked forward to
proving him wrong because he was arrogant
and vicious and he was always trying to get
fresh with her. He probably wouldn't believe
her, anyway, but some of the others would.
Terry would.

She looked at her watch and saw that it
was twenty to eleven; her mother would have
set off for church. It sickened her to think
of her mother in church reciting Christian
prayers about charity and brotherly love. It
was the kind of hypocrisy Terry complained
about — people who were always saying one

thing and doing another. Like the politicians. Still, her mother did a lot of hard work for the Church Bazaars; that was something.

Veronica could hear the radio faintly from next door — Mick Jagger singing an old hit:

". . . here it comes, my nineteenth nervous breakdown . . . here it comes . . ."

And here comes my twentieth, thought Veronica, if that damn door is still locked. She jumped out of bed and found the door was open. Outside on the landing was her transistor, an electric light bulb, a glass of milk, and a plateful of jam sandwiches. She knew that her father had made them because they were oozing with jam. Her mother always scraped it on so thinly that you could hardly taste it.

Veronica took the key out of the door and replaced it on the inside, then took the things into her room. She switched on the transistor and found Mick Jagger, then drank the whole glass of milk in one gulp. Gobbling the sandwiches, she felt happy and hopeful. Her mother would be on her way to church by now and she decided to go out to the workshop for another talk with her father; he always worked on his ships on Sunday mornings. She wanted to know what her mother had said to him about her the night before.

Veronica ran across the sunny yard to the shed and opened the door. "Can I come in?"

Her father was sitting on a stool in the corner by his bench, carving a piece of wood, and he looked up at her with his sad, gentle smile. He wore an old brown overall that was too big for him and had to have the cuffs turned back.

"Found your sandwiches, all right?" he said. "Had enough, have you?"

"Yes, thanks, Daddy, they were gorgeous. Gorgeously jammy."

He went on carving and she hoisted herself up on to his bench, among the sawdust and shavings.

"Don't dirty yourself now, pet," he said.

"No — I've only got my old jeans on." She knew she mustn't ask him anything yet. He hated being hustled.

Veronica adored the tiny workshop. The ceiling was laced with dusty cobwebs and there was a wonderful smell of new wood and pipe tobacco. Most of all, there were the ships — more than twenty of them —galleons like the ones in the Spanish Armada. They were crowded on shelves and propped along the window ledge; there would soon be no more room for them in the shed. It was a problem to know what he would do when this happened, because her mother would never have them in the house. She was always taunting him about his "stupid boats."

They were only about a foot long but he made them to scale from detailed plans and they were all carved and painted so perfectly that if Veronica made her fist into a peephole and looked at one, shutting out everything else, she could almost imagine it was real. What she liked best were the brightly coloured figureheads, and the tiny coils of string her father arranged on the decks to look like rope.

At last she said, "Tell me about last night, Daddy. What did she say about Terry?"

He blew the dust from the tiny oar he was carving and put it down carefully on the bench. Then he took a pipe out of the pocket of his overall and began to fill it from his tobacco pouch. It was a red leather one Veronica had given him for Christmas, paid for out of her earnings at the hairdresser's.

"We had a bit of trouble," he said. "I may as well tell you. She was dead against Terry, of course, because of his long hair and everything — and she thinks you're too young to go with boys anyway. Then there was the mini-skirt. She said you looked like a tart." He struck a match and lit his pipe.

"Oh, Daddy — she didn't! Everybody wears them — you know they do."

"Of course — of course. I'm just telling

you what she said. She wanted me to forbid you to see Terry again, but I wouldn't agree. I told her I thought she was mistaken about the whole thing and that you were behaving just like any normal girl of your age."

"Good for you, Daddy! Thanks."

"But it's terribly difficult for me, Veronica. You must try and understand. She's jealous, you see — jealous of the way I take your side against her. That's always made a lot of trouble between us. In fact it's one of the reasons she's so — so unkind to you."

"Poor Daddy!" Veronica saw the pink patches flame at the sides of his jaws and she knew that she was beginning to understand adult problems as never before. She saw what a painful position her father was in, and she also felt, for the first time, a queer pang of sympathy for her mother, jealous and middle-aged and neurotic, unloved by her husband and her daughter. There was no doubt that she *was* unloved, and although it was her own fault, that didn't make it any better. In fact it probably made it worse. . . .

"What shall I do, then?" asked Veronica uncertainly. She slid off the bench and began to play with the little oar that lay among the shavings.

"Well, I think you should be free to live your own life — sensibly and wisely, as I know you will. I'd like to meet your Terry and I'd like to invite him here, but I'm afraid that's out of the question, so ——" He sucked at his pipe, which had gone out.

"Yes?"

"So just carry on as you have been, pet. Be good and enjoy yourself — only don't tell your mother I said so, for heaven's sake."

Veronica put her arm round her father's neck and kissed his rough cheek. "What would I do without you?" she said.

"You don't have to," he told her. "But I'll tell you one thing."

"What?"

"I should get out of here quickly before your mother comes back from church!"

7

The Youth Club had once been a small pri-
vate infants' school and you could still see the
traces of childish scribbles through the pale
green distemper on the walls. The Recrea-
tion Room was known as Ringo's Room; two
sisters with a passion for Ringo Starr had dec-
orated it and christened it when the Club was
first opened. The girls had since moved to
another town but the name had stuck, and
the Club itself was known as "Ringo's."

There was a life-size picture of its name-
sake over the mantelpiece, and one wall was
adorned with photographs of pop groups,

singers, and disc jockeys. The floor was covered with new red lino but all the furniture was old. Against one wall was a row of ancient armchairs, and under the window — which looked out on to an Ante-natal Clinic (much to everyone's amusement) — was a brown leather sofa with the stuffing bursting out of the seams. Next to it was a bookcase of tattered paperbacks and a table littered with magazines. In the far corner stood a piano. It had been quite tuneful until Jeremy Wright emptied a plateful of egg and chips into the works. In front of the fireplace was a thick handmade rug in fiery reds and pinks which had been donated by Terry's mother, and this was where Terry used to sit cross-legged when he sang his strange off-beat songs.

Veronica arrived at the Club at a quarter to three. She had, of course, left the house before her mother returned from church; her father had given her the money for a snack lunch in the town. He said he would try to persuade her mother to let her stay on at the Club where her friends were.

She hung her white coat in the hall and went into the cloakroom to comb her hair. She looked glamorous and sexy in her new skirt with a pale blue angora sweater and silver necklace, but she felt so nervous as she

51

went into Ringo's Room that she almost hoped Terry wouldn't be there. There were about a dozen people in the room but she couldn't see Terry. Dolly Frost was waving mournfully at her from the sofa under the window. She was munching a Mars Bar and playing rummy with a beautiful Jamaican girl called Emilia. Veronica sat on the arm of the sofa, pretending to watch the game and a few minutes later she felt a light touch on her shoulder and looked up into Terry's smiling face.

"Hi!" he said.

"Oh, hullo." She knew she was blushing and she pretended to be interested in her cards, letting her hair swing forward to shield her hot cheeks from his gaze.

He said, "How about coming for a drive? Mother's lent me the car. We could go to the Plain and see the gliding."

"O.K. Thanks." Veronica tossed back her hair and stood up, smoothing her red mini-skirt. Her knees were shaking.

"Ta-ra, Dolly. Ta-ra, 'Milia."

Emilia smiled her brilliant smile and Dolly looked up briefly, her mouth smeared with chocolate. "Cheerio," she said bleakly. "If you can't be good, be careful."

Veronica wished she could laugh with her usual gaiety. But somehow she couldn't.

The car was parked outside the Club — an old blue convertible with the hood down.

"Roll on, next March," said Terry as he slung Veronica's coat onto the back seat. "I'll have the deposit for an M.G. sports saved up by then."

"What make is this?" Veronica asked h She didn't know much about cars.

"Sunbeam. Old as the hills but goes like bomb. Mother adores it — she'll keep it till it drops to bits."

It wasn't until they were out of the town-centre and driving along a wide suburban road that Terry spoke about the previous afternoon.

"I didn't really expect to see you today," he said. "What happened after I'd gone?"

"She locked me in my room — with nothing to eat till this morning. I was starving."

"Christ! How old does she think you are — sixteen or six?"

"I know. And she took the damn bulb out of the light so I couldn't read."

Terry glanced at her with a frown. "That's *really* sick! Poor Ronny. What's the trouble, then? I mean all that she said to me? What goes on for Pete's sake? What did I do — besides not getting a haircut?"

"You didn't do anything. It was me — she's always had it in for me. Thing was, I told her

I was going to the pictures with Dolly Frost. I had to 'cos she says I mustn't go out with boys ——"

"You're joking!"

"I wish I were. There's this skirt, too — she thinks it's miles too short."

"Well, I think it's a knockout!" He touched her knee for a moment and smiled.

"Yeah. Well, it was quite expensive, too. But she thinks I look like a tart in it. That's what she told Dad."

"A tart! *You!* You're the classiest bird at the Club!"

"Oh, I'm not! But that's what she said."

For a while they drove in silence, their hair flying back in the wind. The country hedges were glittering with fresh spring leaves and the white ribbon of road came shooting under the bonnet, dazzlingly bright in the sunshine.

Then Veronica said, "I wouldn't care so much if she was *nice*, Terry. I mean if she was genuinely old-fashioned like my granny, for instance — but she isn't. She's absolutely — *horrible!*"

"Yeah, I could see that," he said soberly. "What's your Pop like?"

"Oh, he's great. He's on my side. But she's just as beastly to him as she is to me, poor darling. The trouble is, he lets her get away with it — he always has done." It was a great relief to pour out her heart to Terry but she was afraid of boring him and decided not to say any more.

"Never mind," he said. "You can leave home when you're seventeen."

"That's not till October. Sometimes I think I can't stick it for another minute."

He drove for a while without speaking, his eyes fixed on the road with calm concentration. Veronica saw that his hands were ingrained with engine grease although he had obviously scrubbed them as clean as he could.

At last he said, "Say, why don't you come and live at our place? My mother's got a boarding house for students. She's a smashing cook."

"But I'm not a student."

"That wouldn't matter. You'd like my mother. She's very kindhearted and she likes pop and trendy gear and everything. The students think she's great. Most of them are at the Polytechnic."

Veronica glanced at Terry's steady profile against the flashing green fields, and the thought of living in the same house was almost too marvellous to contemplate. To leave home . . . to get away from her mother. . . . She'd hate leaving her father, but she wouldn't be too far away; Terry lived somewhere at the other side of the park.

"Yeah," she said. "That might be an idea. Thanks."

She watched the speedometer tremble up to seventy and snuggled back in the comfortable seat, loving the clean air that stung her cheeks and whipped back her hair into a wild silky tangle.

"Not too fast for you, is it?" asked Terry.

"No — it's gorgeous." She thought how kind he was to ask; some boys would have taken pleasure in giving her a fright.

Suddenly she said, without meaning to, "Terry, I *do* think you're sweet."

He didn't answer but she saw his expression soften. The speedometer dropped to sixty, to forty, to twenty, to five. . . .

He parked the car on the grass under a beech tree. A bough of lime-green leaves, transparent and luminous in the sun, was pressing against the windscreen like a bower.

He put his arm round her shoulder and caressed the back of her neck under the tumble of chaotic hair. His large brown eyes, soft as velvet, were fixed on her face, but she hardly dared to look at him.

"I think I'm falling in love with you," he said.

"Me too." Her voice was a kind of squeak, the way it came out.

"*Honest?*"

She nodded.

"Do you want to bother with the gliders today?" he asked her.

"Not really. Not unless you do."

"I don't," he whispered.

And a moment later he was kissing her as she had never been kissed in her life.

8

Veronica had never known that kissing could be so blissful and so exciting; Terry was passionate yet gentle and right at the start he said something that made her happiness complete.

"You know you don't have to be afraid, don't you, Ronny? You know I'd never try to do anything you didn't want."

"Yes. Thanks." There was no way of telling him how grateful she was and how much more she loved him for saying it.

After a while he put up the car hood and they clung together on the back seat while the sun dropped to the treetops and the bough of beech leaves, twitching in the breeze, became a dark silhouette against the windscreen. Passing cars seemed as remote as comets in the sky; there was nothing for Veronica but that secret little world, smelling of old leather and petrol and Terry's newly washed green jersey and her own Coty scent, with the strong comforting feel of his arms around her.

He told her that his father had died eleven years before and his mother had sold their London home and bought the boarding house at Blackford.

"My dad was super," he said. "He was a racing driver — that's how he died — in a crash at Silverstone ——"

"Oh, God!"

"Yeah. A wheel came off when he was doing about a hundred and twenty."

"I don't know how you can bear to be a car mechanic after that," said Veronica.

"Oh, I've always been crazy about cars. I'd like to race, really, but it wouldn't be fair to Mother, not after what happened to Dad. You've got to face it — it's a chancy business."

"I'm glad you aren't going to do anything dangerous," she said, snuggling more closely into his arms.

There was another timeless age of kissing and caressing, then Terry said, "You'll get on fine with Mother. She isn't fussy or possessive or anything. She's just great."

"It must be marvellous to have a mother

you can really love," said Veronica wistfully. "I can't help feeling guilty about mine. I hate her, you know. I really do."

"It's rotten luck but you don't need to feel guilty, just because she's your mother. Nobody'd expect you to love her if she was your next-door neighbour, would they? A person's got to *deserve* to be loved."

"Yeah, but there's that bit in the Bible about 'honour thy father and thy mother.' Doesn't that mean you ought to honour them whatever they're like?"

"Does it make sense. How can you honour your mother when she's doing just the things the Bible says you shouldn't do. You can try to understand why she's so beastly, but you don't have to love her just because she's your mother. Not the way I see it, anyway."

"Oh, I'm so glad you think that, Terry, because I've always felt I was wicked. I can remember saying in my prayers when I was little: 'Please God forgive me for not loving Mummy.' "

"I honestly don't think you need to feel like that. It's like patriotism. You're always taught you should back up your own country just because it's your country, however much you hate what it's doing. Like Vietnam, for instance."

"And if you protest they treat you like dirt.

It makes me sick." She leaned her head on his shoulder and sighed.

He stroked her hair gently and rocked her in his arms. "You make me love-sick," he said.

"Darling Terry. . . ."

"Darling, beautiful Ronny. . . ."

"I'm hungry," said Terry. "Let's go back to my place. Mother won't mind — it's easy on Sundays because she doesn't do supper for the students — just for us. There's always plenty."

"Are you sure?"

"Course. It's terribly free-and-easy."

"I'm shy." Veronica took out her comb and began to tug at the long tangled skeins of her hair.

"You needn't be. Nobody's ever shy with Mother for long. She'll love you."

Mrs. Marchmont's boarding house was called Holly Lodge and stood at the top of a steep hill overlooking the park. Terry left the car in the drive and took Veronica round the back way.

It was an ugly old place with peeling green paint and ramshackle additions built on all round it — greenhouse, shed, porch, garage. The garden was wild and untended, with for-get-me-nots and daffodils growing among the parsley.

The back door was open and they went into a huge untidy kitchen which smelt deliciously of roast pork and sage-and-onion stuffing. The room was deserted, although a transistor radio was emitting *Pick of the Pops* at full blast.

"Mum!" shrieked Terry, above the noise of the Kinks.

There was no answer. Terry turned off the Kinks and called again. Veronica stood demurely in the doorway with her coat over her arm and her bag over her shoulder. Her knees were shaking again.

"Mum! Where are you?"

A distant voice, rich and fruity, came echoing from another part of the house.

"I'm in the bog — shan't be a minute!"

"She spends hours in there," said Terry. "Reads all the time. The place is like a lending library."

"What does she read?"

"Novels mostly. She's writing one as well, only she likes to keep it dark. Actually it's quite good. All about motor racing."

"But how *can* she?" gasped Veronica.

"Getting it out of her system, I suppose. Lots of people write about their troubles, don't they? It's a sort of cure."

"Really? P'raps I'd better write a book about my mother, then!"

Veronica heard the flushing of the lavatory, the running of taps, the slam of a door, and the patter of brisk footsteps. At last Mrs. Marchmont appeared, carrying a library book.

She was a plump little blonde with wispy hair like a baby's and a wide curving mouth bright with lipstick. She was wearing a short orange dress with a gold chain belt. She could easily have been in her twenties, although Terry had said she was thirty-eight.

"Had to finish that chapter," she said to Terry, tossing the book on to the draining board. She obviously had not seen Veronica.

"Mother, this is Ronny. Veronica Mason. We've been for a drive and I've brought her in for supper. Is that O.K.?"

Mrs. Marchmont swung round in surprise and waved across from the sink, smiling broadly. Her eyes were large and velvet brown, like Terry's.

"Glad to see you, dear — of course it's O.K. Come on in. Terry told me about yesterday. Hope you aren't going to get into trouble for coming here."

"I would if my mother found out," she replied, "but Dad's on my side, thank goodness." It was perfectly easy to talk to her; Veronica had never seen a friendlier face.

Mrs. Marchmont nodded. "D'you like pork?" She opened the oven and stuck a fork into a roast potato. "Soon be ready. I've just got to boil the sprouts. They're all washed."

"Can I help?" said Veronica. She liked housework and often cooked the Sunday dinner when her mother was at church.

"Sure. Here, have a pinny. You can wash up those few dishes while I see to the sprouts. Goodness, child, what fabulous legs you've got! You could go on the Folies Bergères with legs like that."

"Don't give her ideas, Mother! want her to stay in Blackford. Matter of fact, we were wondering if she could come and live here later on — in October maybe, when the new session starts?"

"Course she could. We'll have some vacancies then. Would your mother let you come, though, Ronny?"

"No, but ——"

"She can please herself when she's seventeen," broke in Terry. "She live where she likes."

"Legally, yes," said Mrs. Marchmont. "But it's not very nice, is it?"

"It's not very nice for her at home, Mother. In fact that's the understatement of the year, isn't it, Ronny? Tell mother what happened to you last night — the light bulb and everything."

When Veronica had finished the story, the washing-up was done and the sprouts cooked.

9

Mrs. Marchmont needed the car to visit a friend after supper, so Terry and Veronica watched a play on television and then they walked the two miles back to Moon Street. They sauntered slowly alongside the park and through the dreary, lamplit streets with their arms round one another, and Veronica was so happy that the problems awaiting her at home seemed trivial compared with the joy of being with Terry.

"I'd better not come too near the house," he said when they reached the end of Moon Street. "I'll get shot if your mother sees me again!"

Veronica groaned. "I feel awful about it," she said. "And specially when your mother's been so sweet to me."

"You can't help it, chick. Where will you say you've been? You couldn't possibly tell her the truth, could you?"

"Lord, no—she'd murder me! I'll say I've been at Dolly Frost's, setting her hair for her."

"Which is your house?" Terry asked her, looking down the dingy terrace. "I like to be able to imagine where you are."

"It's Number 5—down on the right, by the streetlamp."

"Is that your bedroom window?"

"No, that's theirs. Mine's at the back—looking over the railway." She sighed. "It's a horrid house, Terry. I'm ashamed of it, really."

"Not with me?"

"Yeah, I am. Not only because it's small and slummy-like, but your place is so gay and cosy inside. Ours isn't. You can't feel at home in it, somehow. Mum's so *fussy*. You can't do a *thing*. If you're reading a book you can't leave it on the table. Poor Daddy gets shouted at if he rumples up a cushion. She's always polishing and dusting—ugh!"

"You'll have to come and live with us—that's a cert."

"Is it a fact you can leave home when you're seventeen?"

"I think so. Before that, the police can yank you back."

"I wish I was seventeen now."

"So do I."

There was a wooden bus shelter at the end of Moon Street and Terry led her inside where it was dark and deserted. He kissed her on the brow, to begin with. Then he kissed her cheeks and her chin and her nose. After that he smoothed back her hair and kissed her ears. Then he held her face between his hands and kissed her on the mouth for so long that she felt almost faint with the joy of it.

At last he said, "You know, I'd have asked you out ages ago only I didn't think you'd come."

"What gave you that idea?"

"You seemed so cool with me."

"I didn't feel cool," she said. That was what came of putting up a screen to hide her feelings.

"Wish I'd known," he said.

"Yeah. Matter of fact I thought you were keen on Jackie."

"She's all right, but she's a selfish little thing. Look how she behaved at the pictures yesterday."

"She's beautiful, though."

"Pretty," said Terry. "Not beautiful. *You're* beautiful."

"Oh, Terry. I'm not!"

"Yes you are. You're special. Your eyes just make me weak."

She felt her cheeks burning with pleasure. "Well, I'm glad. I think you're smashing, too. I always have."

He took the long curtains of her hair in his hands and gravely tied them under her chin, like a scarf. "Ronny, I wish to God you didn't have to lie to your mother about us. It's so damn stupid. You aren't doing anything wrong — except the lying itself."

"I know — but what else can I do? She forces me into it, doesn't she? I've always had to tell her lies — there was no other way."

"It's rotten for you," he said.

She looked up at him and tried to smile. "Oh, she can go take a running jump — I don't care." But she did care, and it was hard to keep the telltale quiver from her voice.

He freed her hair and kissed her again, holding her so tightly that she was breathless. A bus was approaching the shelter, and the headlights suddenly flooded over them.

Veronica drew quickly away from him. "I'd better go now. I'll see you tomorrow at Ringo's — if I'm still alive!"

"Bye, then. Good luck!"

Veronica walked away down Moon Street. The bus was drawing up at the stop and she turned and saw Terry standing there, waving, in the glare of the headlights. She waved back, feasting her eyes on the sight of him, unwilling to turn away.

It was then that she saw a woman getting off the bus, a small woman in a checked coat, with a headscarf tied under her chin. The woman looked at Terry and then she followed his eyes and saw Veronica. Her glasses flashed in the lights of the bus. It was Mrs. Wainwright.

Veronica turned and began to walk quickly towards her home. She was sure that Mrs. Wainwright would tell her mother what she had seen and she felt a cold sickness inside her. She could imagine the squeaky little voice: "I saw that girl of yours waving to a boy at the bus stop — one of these long-haired ruffians he was, too. . . ." And then her mother would get Mrs. Wainwright to describe him and it would be obvious that it was Terry — tall and slender, with his blond wavy hair and blue anorak. It was incredibly bad luck that she should get off that very bus, but Veronica remembered that she always went to read to a blind old lady on Sunday nights. She began to walk more slowly as she considered this. It was kind of Mrs. Wainwright to turn out every week like that; after all, she didn't have to. She must be a decent person in some ways. Would it be a good idea, perhaps, to explain to her about Terry and try to win her over?

Veronica could hear footsteps behind her in the empty street. She knew it was Mrs.

71

Wainwright because she walked with a limp. Suddenly she made up her mind to speak to her. She turned and saw her hobbling up the opposite side of the terrace towards her own house. Her face was almost hidden by her headscarf and the big horn-rimmed spectacles.

Veronica hurried across the road. "Excuse me — could I —"

Mrs. Wainwright gave a little squeak of alarm. "Oh-h! You frightened me, child. Whatever's the matter?"

"Can I talk to you a minute, please?"

"What's this? What's the matter?" She hunched herself more deeply into her coat, almost as if she was afraid of Veronica. "I saw you waving to that boy, so don't you think I didn't. Is that the one you went to the pictures with yesterday? I don't know what your mother'll say — I really don't. I think it's —"

"Just a sec — that's what I want to tell you about. He's terribly sweet — really he is. Mother doesn't understand, that's all. *Please* don't tell her you saw me with him — it'll only make trouble."

"Make trouble! Make trouble!" The puffy little face was crisscrossed with angry lines as she glared at Veronica. "It's *you* that's making trouble with your lying and disobedience. Coming to me behind your mother's back, asking favours. You ought to be ashamed of yourself."

"But I just wanted to *explain* ——"

"I don't want to hear another word. Suppose your mother was to look out of her window and see me talking to you like this! What would she think about that? She'd think I was taking your part against her, wouldn't she? You youngsters don't look further than the ends of your noses — no thought for other people. Self, self, self, all the time." She began to move away. "Now don't you come to me with your explanations, as you call them. Take them to your mother — she knows what's best for you."

"But I *can't* — she doesn't *understand*. She doesn't even *want* to understand!" Veronica was trembling with frustration and for a moment she thought she saw a fleeting look of sympathy on Mrs. Wainwright's face. But it was only for a moment and then she limped away without saying another word.

Veronica slowly crossed the road, kicked a broken milk bottle that was lying in the gutter and made her way miserably towards Number 5.

10

Her mother was waiting for her in the hall.

"And where have *you* been, might I ask? Do you know what time it is?"

Veronica inspected her watch very closely. "Thirteen and a half minutes to eleven."

"Didn't I say you must always be in by ten-thirty at the latest?"

"Daddy thinks it should be eleven-thirty, now that I'm earning."

Mrs. Mason compressed her lips into a thin line of fury. "Will you stop bringing your father into every argument. He's been going on at me all day about this Club of yours. I'm sick to death of it. Have you been there again tonight?"

"No, I haven't. But there's nothing wrong with it. It's a smashing Club. And it's run by a schoolmaster, if you want to know."

"That doesn't mean anything. There's plenty of schoolmasters no better than the young thugs they're supposed to be teaching. You haven't seen that boy again, have you?" Mrs. Mason leaned forward, her hands clenched at her sides, and Veronica thought once again how much like a crow she looked. For a moment she hesitated. She wanted to cry out, *Yes, I have — and I'm not ashamed of it — and I won't lie about it because it's too marvellous and beautiful to lie about . . .* but she dared not tell the truth. Instead, she muttered in a low voice, "No, I've been to Dolly's — she wanted her hair setting."

"And how do you expect me to believe a word you say after yesterday?"

"Please yourself — I don't care."

"Don't speak to me like that! You'll care soon enough if I see you with that long-haired lout again!"

"Terry is not a lout." Veronica felt sick. She turned away towards the staircase. She had to get to her room, get away from this terrible argument which would drive her to tears in a minute unless she could escape.

Her mother gripped the sleeve of her coat. "*Now* where do you think you're going?" She pulled her away from the stairs. "I haven't finished with you yet. What have you been saying to your father about this Club? Does this boy Terry belong to it?"

Veronica did not reply.

"*Does he?*"

"Yes. But so does Dolly and lots more of my friends. If I don't go there what am I supposed to do in the evenings? You won't let me watch what I want on the telly, and I can't have my friends here because you say they make the house untidy. What do you expect me to *do* — sit in my room every night reading a book? Or go to evening classes and learn Spanish? You'll have to let me go out with boys *some* time, won't you? Unless I'm going to be a nun! You don't *want* me to have a good time, do you, that's what it is!" She stopped for lack of breath, and stared at her mother's white face. "And what's more," she went on, "I'm jolly well not leaving the Club, whatever you say!"

"Go to your room this minute!"

"No, I won't. I'm not going to my room just when you say so, like a bloody baby."

"I said *go to your room!*"

"No!" Veronica stood firm, though her knees were trembling so violently that she could hardly stand. A second later, her mother struck her across the face, a stinging blow that brought the tears to her eyes.

She raced into the kitchen and saw that the light was still shining from her father's workshop. She switched on the kitchen light and ran to the back door. "*Daddy!*" she shrieked. Her mother pulled her back but she saw the workshop door swing open and her father came running towards the house. He burst into the kitchen, his face haggard with alarm.

"What is it?" he cried. "What's happened?" He was wearing his baggy brown overall with the cuffs turned back and there were wood-shavings clinging to his sleeve.

Veronica flung herself into his arms but he did not embrace her. She thought, He daren't even be kind to me when she's there—he's *afraid* of her. . . .

Her mother said, "You daughter is insolent and disobedient. She has openly defied my authority. What are you going to do about it?"

"What's this, Veronica?" His eyes, unused to the bright kitchen light, blinked at her in an anguish of misery and uncertainty.

"I've told her I'm not leaving the Club," said Veronica. "And I won't go up to my room when she tells me to. I'm old enough to do as I like—that's what you said this morning, isn't it, Daddy?"

There was a long moment of silence. Then Mrs. Mason said icily, "I see. So you've taken her side against me, as usual."

"No, dear — I just said ——"

"You *know* she's a liar, George. You *know* she lied about going to the pictures with that boy yesterday ——"

"You *forced* me to, didn't you?" broke in Veronica. "I'd never have lied if you'd been reasonable. I hate lying — it makes me feel sick. I want to tell the truth all the time but how *can* I when you won't let me go out with boys or anything ——"

Her father broke in, "Veronica — Ethel — couldn't we try to break down the barriers — all of us. Can't we all tell the truth and be honest — try to understand each other a bit better?"

"I agree," said Veronica. "I think that's a very good idea." She felt a surge of strength building up inside her, but it was a wicked kind of strength because she knew that she herself, and her father, had little to hide, whereas her mother could not be honest without confessing to a great deal of unkindness. She went on, "I'll start, shall I, Daddy? I'm not going to tell any more lies — I'm going to tell the absolute truth. O.K.?"

Her father put out his hand and patted her

shoulder. "Just a minute, Veronica. Don't let's be hasty, eh? Just let's ——"

"I'm not being hasty. I just want to be *honest*, like you said." She turned to her mother and squared her shoulders. "I've been with Terry all the time today," she announced. "I love him and I'm going to go on seeing him whatever anyone says. How about that?" It was a relief to get it out, and in any case Mrs. Wainwright would have told her.

Her father said shakily, "Well, at least you've been honest, Veronica. I'm sure it's better that way — don't you think so, Ethel?"

Veronica looked at her mother and saw that the thin features had frozen into a mask of loathing. "What does it matter to you what I think? It never has mattered, has it? You've always taken her side against me."

"And why do you think that is?" cried Veronica. "It's because you've always been horrible about everything I wanted to do. You've never listened to my point of view. Never. It's always been the same — if I don't do what you tell me to do, you hit me. Just like to-night —— "

"Is that true, Ethel? Did you hit her?" He was looking distractedly from Ethel to Veronica and back to Ethel again.

"It was only a tap," said her mother. "If

she behaves like a spoilt child she must expect to be treated like one."

"I'm not a child — that's just where you're wrong. Lots of girls are *married* at my age."

"Of course you're a child — don't be ridiculous. Just because some great lout takes you to the pictures you think you're grown-up, don't you? If you could see how idiotic you look — going around half naked, with your hair all over your face. Call yourself a hairdresser! A tart — that's what you look like. Don't get the idea that any boy wants you for anything but a bit of cheap sex!"

"*Ethel* — for heaven's sake! Don't be so unkind."

"*Unkind!*" Her mother's voice was like the crack of a gun. "Listen to *you* — taking her part against me! Isn't *that* unkind?"

Veronica's heart was hammering as if it would burst. For a few moments no words would come, and then she gasped out, "I think you're the . . . rottenest mother that . . . anybody ever had!" She raced out of the kitchen into the hall and up the dark stairs. Behind her she heard her father calling, "Veronica — come back and say you're sorry," but she only wanted to escape, to die, to cry, to be alone. And in any case, she wasn't sorry. . . .

She slammed the bedroom door behind her and turned the key in the lock. One thing was

shop; her mother never went in there, so far as she knew.

Darling Daddy,

I've got to leave home. I can't stand her for another day. Don't worry about me. I'll be all right. Terry's mother runs a boarding house so I can stay there, I expect. Try not to let mother come after me at work or anything. She won't want to, anyway — she'll be glad to get rid of me. Mrs. Marchmont is an angel so you honestly needn't worry, and please don't try to make me come home. If you want to see me, you can always find me at Irene's.

Love from Veronica

It was nearly midnight by the time she had finished, but her parents had not come to bed. They were still arguing in the kitchen; she could hear the sound of their voices. She got undressed, put on her pink woollen dressing gown and went out onto the landing, straining to hear what they were saying. The kitchen door was closed but she could hear her mother's grating voice quite distinctly. Cautiously she crept halfway down the stairs, holding her breath when they creaked, and sat there, listening.

"So you think I'm unbalanced?" her mother

was saying. "So you think I've been unbalanced ever since Nigel was killed?"

"Yes, I do, Ethel. I really do. All this persecution of Veronica when the poor kid's done nothing to deserve it —— "

"I think she's done a great deal to deserve it."

"Nonsense. You couldn't have a sweeter child."

Veronica's throat ached. Darling Daddy....

"*Sweet?*" cried her mother. "Don't you hear the insolent way she talks to me?"

"Of course I do, but it's only because you treat her so unreasonably. She doesn't talk to me like that, does she?"

Veronica crept further down the creaking stairs and sat there tensely, hugging her knees to keep warm. This conversation was not to be missed.

Her father was saying, "If only you'd try to understand her, be on her side. That's all she wants — just to feel that you're on her side. That's what *all* kids want."

"And how about *you* being on *my* side? Don't you think that's what *I* want!"

"Of course — of *course*, I understand. Believe me, I do. But I can't be on your side if you keep on making Veronica unhappy, can I? Oh, Ethel — couldn't you admit it — admit you've been wrong — make a fresh start. I'd help you all I could, you know I would!"

Veronica waited breathlessly for her mother's response. If only she *would* break down and confess how unkind she's been! It could be the start of a new life for all of them. But Veronica didn't expect it. She had never heard her mother cry — or really laugh, for that matter. She didn't seem capable of letting go, or of seeing anybody's point of view but her own.

Now Mr. Mason was repeating what he'd said before. "I'd help you all I could, Ethel. Why don't you let me help you?"

"When did you ever help me?" she cried. "When did you ever do anything for me at all! Keeping me in this miserable hovel of a place, setting my own daughter against me, leaving me alone every night of the week while you scratch away in that filthy shed with your stupid little boats. Help me, indeed!"

"You've driven me away from you, Ethel — there's never been any joy in the house since — since —— "

"Since Nigel died? Why don't you say it? And whose fault is it that Nigel isn't alive today? Whose fault is it that Nigel isn't a lovely boy of thirteen looking after his mother —— "

"Ethel — for God's sake —— "

Veronica leaned forward, listening intently so as not to miss one word of this dramatic dialogue. She thought, Whose fault does

Mother think it is, then? Is she blaming poor old Daddy for that as well? She tucked her bare feet under the hem of her dressing gown to keep warm, and leaned her head against the banisters.

There was a long silence and then she heard her mother's voice, rasping and hard. "I'm going to tell Veronica about Nigel."

"Ethel — no — no — *please!*"

"Yes, I am. It's time she knew the truth. I've kept it quiet too long."

Kept what quiet? thought Veronica, leaning forward so eagerly that she almost topped downstairs.

Now she heard her father's voice, raised in g at distress. "But you promised you'd *never* te her — never as long as you lived."

Maybe I did — but it was only because you for ed me to. You said you'd leave me for goo if I told her, didn't you? That was it, was t it? Well, that was a long time ago. You can ave me tomorrow, for all I care. I'm going to tell her."

"Ethel — you'd never forgive yourself if you told her now, after all these years. It would be so cruel — so dangerous."

"What do you mean — dangerous?"

"She might take it terribly to heart — you *know* how highly strung she is."

Veronica's heart was thumping so loudly

that she could hardly hear the voices from the kitchen. She was terrified of what she might hear but she was compelled to go on listening. She almost stopped breathing as her mother spoke again.

"It's time she knew. Maybe she'll repent of her ways when she understands the wicked thing she did."

"Wicked? You must be mad! How can a child of three be wicked? She had no *idea* what she was doing."

Her mother gave a bitter laugh. "Ha — listen to you! She can do no wrong in your eyes, can she? Never could."

"Ethel — you'll have to see a doctor. I'll fix it up tomorrow. You're talking the most terrible rubbish — you really must get medical attention. It isn't fair to any of us, going on like this."

"I'm seeing no doctor. And I'm telling that girl the truth about Nigel first thing tomorrow morning."

"You really mean it, don't you?"

"Of course I mean it. You try to stop me."

"I won't try to stop you," said her father. "Only I think it would be better coming from me, if you don't mind. I'll tell her myself."

"Tell her, then. But I'll see she knows the truth — so don't think you can fob her off with some airy-fairy story of your own."

"I'll tell her now. I'll wake her up and tell her this very minute."

"Go on, then. Get out of here. Look at all the mess you've brought in — bits of wood and sawdust all over my floor. I'll have to clean it up, now — I'll have to wash this floor before I go to bed."

Veronica heard her father give a groan of disgust and then she heard his footsteps approaching the kitchen door. She just had time to race up the stairs to her room and avoid being seen.

12

Veronica managed to get into bed and pretend to be asleep before her father knocked on the bedroom door. She didn't answer at first but when he knocked more loudly, she called out, "Come in! with convincing drowsiness. He came in and sat on the bed. There was moonlight coming through the window and he didn't switch on the light; she was relieved about this because she was afraid he might notice the signs of her packing. She had pushed the suitcase under the bed and put the letter in her bag, but the top of the dressing table was empty, which looked suspicious, and there was a pile of shoes on the floor which she couldn't get into the case.

"I'm sorry to wake you," he said gently, "but I've got to talk to you."

She rubbed her eyes. "What is it?" She would have liked to confess that she had been eavesdropping on the stairs but she was ashamed of it and did not want him to know.

"It's just something I want to explain to you myself — before your mother tells you about it."

She dreaded what she would hear, but in the darkness it was easy to pretend to be sleepy and irritable. "What are you talking about?" she grunted.

"It's about — about Nigel," said her father shakily. "You see, when he died I made your mother promise not to tell you how it happened, because it was — well, it was something to do with you."

Veronica held her breath. Her heart was beating so heavily she was sure he must be able to hear it.

"It was nothing you could help," he went on. "You were only three, as you know, but it was something you did —— "

"You mean — it was my fault he died?" broke in Veronica.

"No — no! I don't mean that at all. It wasn't anybody's fault — it was just an accident."

"What happened?" said Veronica. She was trembling all over.

"You were playing with a ball in the park. Nigel was in his pram and your mother was sitting on a seat — reading, I think. Anyway, the ball rolled under the pram and stuck there — it was a big beach ball — and when you pulled at it to get it out, you must have moved the brake. The pram went running away down a slope and crashed into a wall. Nigel was thrown out and killed."

Veronica drew a deep breath and let it out again. She felt strangely relieved. She hadn't done anything wicked, like her mother said. *Any* child could move a pram brake by accident getting a ball out.

"Why are you telling me now?" she said. She felt quite cross with relief. "What do you want me to do — say I'm sorry? Or what?"

"Of course not, pet. It wasn't your fault at all — not the tiniest bit. It was just a childish accident. But your mother was determined to tell you about it and blame you for it. She was so angry about Terry and everything. Anyway I had to come and explain the truth to you first. You mustn't take any notice of the things she says, Veronica. She's sick — mentally sick. She'll have to see a doctor."

Veronica sat up in bed and stared at her father. His face was just a black silhouette against the moonlit window. "Does she really blame me — when I was only *three?*"

"I don't know," he said. "I think it's all jealousy, really — because I'm so fond of you and — let's face it — not so fond of her. But whatever it is, it's terribly sad because it's made us all so unhappy — your mother most of all, I expect."

"Well, she deserves to be unhappy," said Veronica. "She never thinks about anybody but herself."

"I know — but maybe that's what mental sickness is, most of the time. Locked up in a tight little selfish world. It must be hell."

"Yes," said Veronica. For a fleeting moment she could guess what it must be like. "Yeah, that's what they mean by hell, I expect."

"It wouldn't have been so bad if she'd had another son," said her father, "but she wouldn't let me near her after Nigel died. So you can see, things haven't been too bright."

"But that's thirteen years ago!" gasped Veronica.

"That's right."

"Poor Daddy." She put her arms round him and nursed his head on her shoulder. "You've had a horrible life, haven't you?"

He began to sob. "It would have been — if it hadn't been for you. You've been my salvation. But I couldn't bear you to blame yourself — about Nigel — "

"I won't, Daddy. I promise I won't. Nobody can help what they do when they're three, can they?"

He took out a handkerchief and blew his nose. "Of *course* not. You're so sensible, you kids. So honest and decent. I see now — it would have been all right to tell you before. That's what I ought to have done. But I threatened to leave your mother if she told you — I thought it might upset you too much."

"I'm glad you told me. It's always best to be honest. I'm glad I told Mother about Terry, as well."

"Don't be too hard on her, will you?"

"O.K., Daddy." She thought, That'll be easy because I won't be here. Thank heaven, I won't be here. I'll be at Terry's.

He stood up. "I think I can hear your mother coming to bed," he whispered. "Good night, pet."

"Good night, Daddy."

When he had gone she lay awake for a long time. She didn't really feel guilty about Nigel but she did feel guilty about leaving home and deserting her father. Still, she couldn't stay with him forever. And in any case, Terry wanted her, too; she was sure he loved her as she loved him, and not in the cheap way her mother had suggested. Her poor mother! No

wonder she hated the park! And yet Veronica
had condemned her for it, not understanding.
It was tragic how little we all understood of
the secret pains in people's hearts — and how
little they understood ours.

She snuggled under the blankets and
thought about the next day. She hoped to
goodness it would be all right to stay at Mrs.
Marchmont's.

MONDAY

13

When she woke up the next morning Veronica felt frightened about leaving home. She wondered if she ought to see Mrs. Marchmont first; she had nowhere else to go, and she dreaded having to come home again once she had left.

For a while she lay in bed and considered unpacking her case and waiting until the next day, but the memory of the previous night came flooding back and she knew that she must go away, whatever happened. If Mrs. Marchmont couldn't have her, she would find a room somewhere and live by herself. What troubled her most was her fear that the police might force her to return to Moon Street; a girl at school had run away from home and a policewoman had taken her back again. . . .

Suddenly she leapt out of bed and dragged her suitcase from underneath. It was no good — she'd got to risk it. She would soon be seventeen and then she could live where she liked. She folded her dressing gown, crammed it in the case, and went to the mirror. Terry had said she was beautiful but she didn't think she was; her nose was too small and her mouth too big. Her eyes were certainly the best thing — large and dove-grey and very wide apart. Still, so long as Terry loved her that was all that mattered. That was all that would ever really matter.

She looked out of the window. In spite of everything, she couldn't help feeling sad about leaving. It was a miserable house but she loved her own room; it had been her secret haven for as long as she could remember. She liked the rumble of the passing trains, the clatter of the signals nearby, the friendly workshop in the little yard below, and the cupboard of childhood treasures which she would, of course, have to leave behind. Worst of all, she would have to leave her father behind.

She heard him calling that he was out of the

bathroom so she washed and dressed as quickly as she could and went downstairs. She felt sick at the prospect of seeing her mother, but at least it wouldn't be for long. In an hour or so she would be leaving the house for good, starting a new and independent life. . . .

Her father was in the kitchen, scraping a slice of burnt toast. "Your mother's got a headache," he said. "She's staying in bed."

"Thank God for that!" said Veronica.

"Veronica!"

"I didn't mean thank God she has a headache — I meant thank God she's staying in bed. Shall I make us some scrambled eggs? Or would you like one of those cheese omelettes with tomato in?" She loved cooking things for her father.

"Just scrambled eggs this morning, pet. I've got to get to the shop extra early because we're expecting the builders in to do some alterations."

He was going off early and her mother was in bed. So Fate was helping her to escape! It would be exceptionally easy for her to slip out the back way with her case and her transistor, leaving the letter in the workshop. Nevertheless, as she went into the pantry for the eggs she could only think that this might be the last breakfast she would cook for her father, and as she whisked the eggs the tears ran down her nose and dropped into the bowl. She mixed them in with the egg and thought how poetic it was that this last breakfast should contain the salt of her own tears.

She longed to tell him she was going, but she dare not because he would be sure to feel it his duty to stop her.

He must have noticed her weepy face as they ate their scrambled eggs but he said nothing about it; he probably thought it was a reaction from the previous night. She made some coffee and when they had finished it she could not bear him to go.

"It's only ten past eight, Daddy. Couldn't you smoke your pipe till twenty past? Or I could make some more coffee."

"No, I must be off now, I'm afraid." He was putting on his coat. "I've got some things to do before these builders arrive." He wasn't even looking at her; he was fastening his belt. "Cheerio, pet. Have a good day."

"Good-bye, Daddy ——" She wanted to fling her arms round his neck and tell him how much she loved him, but he was waving at the door and she could only watch him cross the yard and vanish through the back gate.

Veronica left her suitcase at the Bus Station luggage office. At six o'clock when she left work, she would go to the Club and see Terry. Then they could take the case on the bus to his place and persuade his mother to let her stay.

The day at Irene's seemed endless. There was the usual depressing Monday-morning atmosphere and Veronica could do nothing right. Her first mistake was to take her transistor to the hairdresser's with her and play Radio One in the cloakroom, her second to spill black hair-dye on the pink carpet and her third to upset a tray of hairpins into a client's lap.

By the time she arrived at the Club, Veronica was sick and nervous and had lost confidence in the whole idea of leaving home and asking Mrs. Marchmont for hospitality.

When she went into Ringo's Room there was no sign of Terry. There were just a few boys playing cards at the table. She picked up a copy of *Petticoat* and leaned against the mantelpiece, watching the door. After a while Jeremy Wright slouched in. He was wearing a handsome blue velvet suit and frilly shirt but his slovenly posture made the clothes look ridiculous. He came over to her, drew on a cigarette, and coughed smoke into her face. "Hello, legs. Where's Terry then? Having it away with Jackie Drake, is he?"

Veronica felt her cheeks begin to burn but

she shrugged her shoulders and pretended to go on reading.

"Come over to the Discotheque," he went on. "You want a bit of hotting up, you do."

She shook her head. "I'm supposed to be meeting Terry."

"Supposed to be, eh? What kind of date's that? Come on, we can pop into the Spotted Dog on the way."

"I can't. I'm under age."

"What does that matter? My sister goes and she's only fourteen. Vodka and lime, she has. She's well-developed, mind. But you're not so bad yourself." He looked brazenly at the fullness under the yellow blouse. "Come on. You and me could go places."

"No, thanks, Jeremy. I'm waiting for Terry."

At that moment the Jamaican girl, Emilia, came in.

"Oh, Veronica — there you are! There's a letter for you on the notice board."

"For me?" Veronica's heart began to thump. Her father would have read her note by now; it could easily be a message from him, ordering her home.

She rushed to the entrance hall and found the letter pinned to the board with a drawing pin. She recognised Terry's strong round writing on the envelope because she had seen copies of his song lyrics. She took the letter into the lavatory and locked the door.

Darling Ronny. Bad news. Mother's in hospital with a broken leg — she had a car crash last night. I'll be at home so please come if you can. I love you. Terry.

14

Terry must have been watching for Veronica out of the window because he opened the front door of Holly Lodge before she rang the bell.

"Oh, Terry ——"

He shut the door and hugged her tightly for a moment, then he said, "It's all right — I've been to see her. She'll be O.K. But she's badly bashed up, poor old girl. Two broken ribs as well as her leg — and masses of cuts and bruises."

"How did it happen?" They went into the living room and sat on the settee where they had watched television the previous evening.

"It wasn't her fault," said Terry. "She's a super driver. Some maniac came belting out of a side turning. He's in hospital, too, and Mother's terribly worried because he might lose the sight of an eye. That's just like Mother — she's far more upset about him than she is about herself."

"She's fantastic — really she is."

"Yeah — she's ever so cheerful. Says she'll have lots of time to get on with her novel. She's worried about things here, though, as you can imagine." He took Veronica's hands and held them tightly. "But what about you, chick? How did you get on last night?"

"Oh, Terry — it was awful. I've so much to tell you." She hesitated, then blurted out, "I've left home!"

"Left home?"

"Yeah. For good."

"But, Ronny — you can't! They'll only fetch you back." He let go of her hands and faced her anxiously.

"They won't, 'cos I'm not going — I don't care what anybody says."

"But the police — they can force you."

"They won't get to know. At least I don't see how. Dad won't tell — he'll understand. I've left him a note. And Mother'll be damn glad to get rid of me. I've left my case at the Bus Station."

"But where are you going to sleep?"

Veronica felt her face going pink. "Well,

that's the trouble — it's a bit difficult now with your mother in hospital."

"You mean you were coming here?"

She nodded. "I was hoping I could have a camp bed or something — till I can move in properly."

"But we're full right up till July. There's sixteen students here now and we've only room for twelve really."

"You don't want me to come," said Veronica in a low voice. She felt sick with disappointment and humiliation. She had expected him to be overjoyed at the thought of having her in the house.

"Don't be silly, Ronny. Of course I do, but —— "

"But what?"

"Well, I feel responsible for you. I don't think you ought to run away from home like that — your parents will be terribly worried."

She stood up angrily and went to the window, looking out at the park with its froth of spring leaves. "You don't *understand*!" she cried. "You don't have a clue what my mother's like! If you knew what she was like you'd *never* say I ought to go back. Just wait till you hear all the things that happened last night. Wait till you hear about my brother Nigel and — and — everything." She was close to tears.

"Come here, chick. I'm sorry." He beckoned her back to the settee. "We'll work something out. And don't get the idea I don't want you here, because I do — I want you here like mad. I'd never have you out of my sight if I could help it!"

"Honest?"

She walked slowly back to the settee and he pulled her onto his knee. "If you only knew!" he said. "How could I possibly not want you here? I love you, you idiot!"

"Then let me stay! I don't care where I sleep. On the floor — anywhere —— "

He kissed her gently, all over her face, then on her lips. "O.K. — we'll go and collect your case from the Bus Station."

"Oh, Terry — thanks!"

"I've told the students they'll have to eat out tonight, but I don't know what the hell's going to happen here while Mother's laid up. She doesn't do lunches but she's on the go all day, cooking and cleaning and looking after everybody. She thrives on it. She does it all herself, you know, except for a cleaning woman on Fridays. She can't afford to have any more help on the rent she charges. She just loves giving the students a nice homely place to live in for next to nothing."

Veronica leapt to her feet so suddenly that she sent him reeling back among the orange cushions on the settee. "Terry!" she cried excitedly, "*I'll* do it! I'll do everything your mother did. I'll run the whole house till she's better again —— "

"Ronny — don't be a twit!"

"I *mean* it — I *mean* it! I can cook — and do housework. I can manage it easily. I'll go and see your mother in hospital and she can tell me exactly what to do. I'd *love* it. Please let me — *please!*"

"But what about your job?"

"They can stuff it. I never wanted to be a hairdresser, anyway. They were horrible to me at Irene's today. I'll make some excuse to leave in a hurry — say I've won the pools or got V.D. or something!"

Terry burst out laughing. "Ronny, you're a peach! A *peach*! Do you really think you can cope with sixteen of them. Eighteen, with you and me. It's a hell of a lot of work, but I'll help you all I can, of course."

"I shall *love* it. I've always wanted to do something really hard and marvellous like this."

"It would be terrific if you could manage it," said Terry. "Mother's worried sick about the students. But you're only a chick — let's face it."

"It doesn't matter, Terry. I'm *determined* to do it — so long as she wants me to."

"Want you to? It'll be such a weight off her mind she'll love you forever." His face suddenly lit up. "Hey!"

"What?"

"Why didn't I think of it before?"

"*What?*"

"You can have Mother's room while she's in hospital."

"Can I really?"

"Of course you can." He got up and put his arms round her. "Ronny, I knew you were great — but not quite so great as this."

He was wearing the same green jersey as the day before, and the newly washed smell of it reminded her of the hours they had spent in the back of the car. She held him tightly and they kissed for a long time, pressing so closely together that she ached with longing for him.

At last they broke away and she smiled shakily, picking one of her long hairs off his jersey. "Look, Terry," she said. "I must get cracking in the kitchen. You go down to the Bus Station and pick up my case, while I get myself organised." She found her bag and gave him the left-luggage ticket.

"O.K. I've cut up the grapefruit for to-morrow's breakfast but I can't find the proper spoons."

"I'll find them," said Veronica. "Don't you worry — I'll look after everything."

"I warn you — the washing up's *colossal* —"

"I don't care."

He turned in the doorway and his great brown eyes were bright with love. "Ronny —"

"Yeah?"

"Marry me one day, will you?"

"Yeah."

He was gone and she went to the window and watched him racing down the road to the bus stop, his fair hair flying, his blue anorak flapping open. He must have known she'd be watching him because he turned and waved. She waved back, pressing her brow against the window, and for the second time that day there were tears running off the end of her nose. Only this time they were tears of exaltation.

15

He had asked her to marry him! They were engaged. At least they were sort of engaged. She felt she had everything she could wish for — except a different mother. Still, you can't have everything, she thought, as she went along the corridor to the kitchen. Most girls seemed to have at least one problem parent; she was lucky her father was such a poppet. Her heart ached when she thought of him at home, worried sick about her departure and probably having a terrible row with her mother at that very moment. Nevertheless, she had no regrets — especially the way things had turned out. Maybe there was some kind of divine plan working through everything if you could only see it. . . . Anyway, the thing to do now was to forget about Number

5, Moon Street and concentrate on making a success of her job at Holly Lodge.

It was marvellous to have that huge kitchen all to herself. She had always enjoyed cooking, and now, with the running of a little boarding house on her shoulders, she could use her talents to the utmost with no one to interfere. She rolled up the sleeves of her yellow blouse, put on Mrs. Marchmont's frilly pink apron, found Radio Luxembourg on the transistor and set to work.

She tidied the kitchen — finding the grapefruit spoons in a box under a pile of tablecloths — and prepared two enormous apple charlottes for the following day. Luckily it was a gas oven she understood, like the one at Moon Street. Then she laid the breakfast tables in the dining room next door, and was glad to see there were four tables for four; this meant that she and Terry would have their meals in the kitchen, as he and his mother had done. It would be almost like being married. Almost. . . .

She heard a crowd of students come in and go clattering upstairs, talking and laughing. It was wonderful to think that they would depend on her as they had depended on Mrs. Marchmont. She was so happy that she found herself dancing to the radio, pirouetting gaily from the sink to the pantry, counting knives and forks to the beat of The Hollies, and feeling as if the torments of the previous night were nothing but a faded nightmare.

By the time Terry arrived back with her case she had a cheese and bacon pie in the oven for the two of them. He lifted her off her feet and swung her round. "Ronny, you're a bloody genius. You've worked wonders already. What smells so good?"

"A pie for our suppers. Put me down and I'll see if it's ready."

"Mother always wanted a daughter," he said, "and she's going to have the peachiest one that ever was!"

"And I'm going to have the peachiest mother-in-law." She put the crisp, golden pie on the table. "*You're* not, though," she added wryly. "You're getting the world's worst. It isn't fair."

She switched off the radio, and as they sat down to supper Terry asked her to tell him what had happened at home the previous night to make her leave.

She described how she had crouched on the stairs and heard her parents arguing, and he listened in silence as he ate his pie, nodding sympathetically from time to time. Then she told him about the beach ball under the pram, and once more he nodded, making no comment except to reassure her that she need not feel guilty about it. It was not until she told him what her father had said about her mother being unbalanced and needing a doctor that he flung down his knife and fork and stared .t Veronica with shining eyes.

"But, Ronny — that's *it* — don't you see? That's why she's always been so rotten to to you. She's sick — mentally sick — because of that baby being killed. She's never got over it, and she blames you — even though it's crazy and nonsensical. Listen, and I'll tell you the way I see it — — "

"You mean what your mother was saying — about there being a reason? You think that's it? Even though I was only *three*?"

"Yeah — well, it's absolutely irrational — but people get like that, don't they? Look at Jeremy Wright at the Club. He's halfway round the bend, I'm sure he is — and it's all because his father drinks too much and beats him up. Remember him putting that plateful of eggs and chips into the piano? It's never been any good since, and yet the funny thing is that old Jeremy loved that piano — he played it jolly well, don't you remember?"

"I didn't know his father was like that." Veronica was remembering Jeremy at the Club that evening, trying to persuade her to go to the Spotted Dog. "O.K. Go on about Mother, then."

"Well, try to see it her way. I reckon she's always been a bit of a difficult character, don't you? I mean unsympathetic and sort of — miserable. I've only seen her that once, but it's in her face, isn't it? Sort of built-in. Well, she falls for your father and they get married. She wants a boy, like you said, but she gets a girl. Your father's dotty about you — and I don't blame him — and he doesn't go much on your mother by now, because he's found out what she's really like. O.K.?"

"Go on," said Veronica. She had to agree with everything he had said so far.

"*So* — she's sick with jealousy, poor woman — right out in the cold, and then at last her dream comes true. She has another baby — and this time it's a boy. Now she's got someone who'll dote on *her* — because boys usually adore their mums, don't they? All her hopes would be pinned on that baby — and then — Bang! He's dead! Bad enough *anyhow* — but it was *you* who did it! You were only a tiny tot and didn't know anything about it, but that wouldn't make any difference when she was half out of her mind with grief. Can't you see how she'd *feel* — specially when she was jealous of you to start with? To be left with no son — just you and your father who were terribly fond of each other and not of her. No wonder she went off her rocker!" He looked at Veronica inquiringly. "Does it make sense?"

She nodded. "I'm sure you're right. You're so wise, Terry. I never understood."

"You're too close to it all — and besides, you've been so unhappy. It's hard to see people's problems when they're making you unhappy."

"Yeah."

She realised she had been too selfishly wrapped up in her own miseries, and although her new understanding could not restore her love for her mother, or make her unkindness any easier to bear, it made her feel a hundred times more forgiving. She now felt an overwhelming sadness for her mother's tragedy.

Terry must have known, because he changed the subject. "That was a smashing pie, Ronny. Where did you learn to cook so beautifully? At school?"

"Yes, and I've always liked making things for Dad. Mother hates cooking — everything she makes tastes funny, somehow. Have an apple."

They each took a shiny red apple from a bowl on the table and began to munch in silence.

Then Veronica said, "When will I be able to visit your mother? I've got to find out what to order from the shops."

"Tomorrow afternoon. Visiting time's two to four."

"Will we tell her — about us, I mean?"

"*Course*. She'll be thrilled. She thinks you're great. She —— "

There was a ring at the front doorbell.

"Oh, Terry — I wonder who that is!" Her heart began to thump.

He got up, still munching the apple. "Don't worry — I expect it's for one of the students."

The front door was too far away for her to hear what was happening and she sat at the table, tense and trembling, with the cold apple clutched tightly in her hand. She was determined to stay at Holly Lodge, whatever happened, and look after everything for Mrs. Marchmont. . . .

It seemed an age before Terry came back, and she knew at once there was something wrong; his face was pale and troubled.

"Your father's here, Ronny," he said. "He won't come in but he says you've got to go back home right away — with all your things. He's got a taxi waiting."

16

Veronica flung down the apple so fiercely that it fell off the table and rolled onto the floor. "I'm not going!" she cried, jumping to her feet and clutching the back of her chair. "Tell him I'm not going."

"You'd better go and see him yourself, chick," said Terry gently. "He was going on about your mother — I couldn't quite make it out. Go and talk to him. He looks all in."

"Oh, Terry, I'm frightened! Suppose he forces me into the taxi or something. Make him come in here and talk to us both. *Please*, Terry! Tell him your mother's in hospital, and all that."

"Yeah. O.K."

When he had gone out Veronica hastily began to peel the potatoes for the next day. Surely her father wouldn't make her go home when he saw what a useful job she was doing at Holly Lodge.

After another long wait she heard footsteps approaching and the two of them came into the kitchen. Her father's face was pallid and he looked very small and old beside Terry.

"Hello, Dad. I'm not coming, so don't try to talk me into it."

"Veronica - you've got to! You don't understand. Your mother's in a terrible state — I've been telling Terry. She's threatening to do some dreadful things if I don't get you back. You'll *have* to come — I'm sorry ——"

"But Terry needs me here, don't you, Terry? His mother's in hospital."

Terry nodded. "I've told your father about all that, Ronny, but I think you'll have to go. It looks as if your mother's on the edge of a breakdown."

Veronica burst into tears. "Don't tell me you're sending me back," she sobbed. "That's all I needed ——"

"You know I want you to stay," said Terry miserably, "but it just seems — if your mother's sick and wants you back ——"

"Wants me back!" screeched Veronica. "She

117

hates my guts. Why should she want me back? Except to torment me again."

Her father said, "She feels terribly guilty — driving you away. I think that's the trouble, really."

"It might not be for long," said Terry. "Just till you sort things out. You've got to be a bit patient if your mother's really sick."

"Come on, Veronica, get your coat," pleaded her father. "The taxi's waiting."

"Send it away, then," cried Veronica, the tears running down her cheeks. "I can't go back — I *can't*! I've got to help Mrs. Marchmont. I'm going to do these potatoes for tomorrow and nobody's going to stop me!"

There was a silence for a while, broken only by the sound of Veronica peeling potatoes and tossing them into a pan of water.

At last her father said in a low voice, "I didn't want to tell you, Veronica, but I'll have to, it seems. Your mother's threatened to do something — something really terrible — if I don't get you home by nine o'clock." There were bright pink patches at the sides of his jaws.

"What? Throw herself onto the railway line?" said Veronica coldly, splashing another potato into the pan.

Terry put his arm round her shoulders. "Ronny — don't be like that! Remember what I was saying over supper. Try and be sympathetic."

She shook him off. "She threatened to do that once before and I was scared stiff. She's *always* threatening horrible things to get me to do what she wants. Well, it won't work anymore, that's all. She said she'd tear up my stamp album if I wore scent. She thinks scent's wicked. Sexy and nasty. Anyway I gave my album to a girl at school so she couldn't harm it. And I still use scent."

Terry turned to Mr. Mason, who was standing by the door, pulling at his tie as if it was strangling him. "What is it she's threatened to do, Mr. Mason?" he asked.

"It's a workshop I've got — in the yard at home. I make model ships in my spare time — galleons, they are — scale models. They're rather a special thing for me and I —— "

Veronica threw down the potato peeler and faced her father with wide eyes, her pulses throbbing. "What about your ships?" she gasped. "What's she going to do to them?"

"She says she'll destroy them if I don't get you home again by nine."

"*What?*" Veronica's voice was a shriek.

"That's what she said — and I'm so afraid she will. She's not herself — I — I've never known her like this before. She's —— "

Veronica looked at her watch and saw that

it was twenty minutes to nine. "Oh God!" she cried. "Oh God — I'll *have* to go back then. Terry — come with us in the taxi — please."

"Yeah. Course I will."

Terry put on his anorak and helped Veronica into her coat and the three of them went to the front door, Terry carrying the suitcase. The sound of a harmonica came echoing from a room upstairs, accompanied by laughter and singing.

Mr. Mason squeezed Veronica's hand as they went down the dark drive to the waiting taxi. "Bless you, pet. I'll make it up to you somehow. I'll make it up to you."

17

The all sat in the back of the taxi with the suitcase beside the driver on the front seat. Veronica was in the middle with Terry on her left. He held her hand tightly but none of them spoke. The driver was a grim-faced fellow with a grey moustache and wild eyebrows. He drove with his elbow sticking out of the window, and muttered to himself from time to time.

Veronica was determined not to stay the night at Moon Street. All she wanted to do was to pacify her mother so as to safeguard the model ships, and then go back to Holly Lodge with Terry and her suitcase. She was longing to finish peeling those potatoes and to make a list of possible meals for the week to show Mrs. Marchmont when she went to visit her the next day. As the taxi made its way down the hill towards the town-centre, she decided to apologise to her mother for being so rude the previous night and to ask — very politely — if she could just stay at Terry's until Mrs. Marchmont was well enough to run the boarding house again.

She remembered one of Terry's songs — a haunting little tune he often sang at the Club. He called it "Bend Like the Willow."

> Give way a little
> When people are tough,
> Only a little
> Can still be enough.
> Be like the willow
> That bends to the breeze;
> The easiest thank you
> Comes after a please.

Terry had proved the value of this philosophy in his dealings with people at Ringo's, and she imagined it was the same at his work. She had often seen him with a group of his garage mates and he was obviously on very friendly terms with them. She now realised that she herself had been the cause of a lot of trouble with her mother. If she had "bent like the willow" a bit more, instead of standing up so stiffly for her rights, half of the belly-aching arguments might have been avoided. And if her mother was mentally sick — as it seemed she was — it was surely up to Veronica to "give way a little" even more readily. After all, she was the strong one, the sane one, the lucky one.

As she sat there in the taxi, wedged between Terry and her father, the two people she loved most in the world, she resolved to be more understanding and try to help her mother to get over her unhappiness. She looked at her watch. It was ten minutes to nine. The driver didn't seem to be driving as fast as he should, and he kept fiddling about with a knob on the dashboard. There was nearly a mile to go, and Veronica was terrified of anything happening to those beautiful little ships.

She nudged her father. "Tell him to hurry," she whispered. "It's ten to."

Mr. Mason nodded but said nothing. Terry squeezed her hand. "Don't worry, chick," he murmured. "We'll make it easily."

But Veronica was trembling with impatience. "Tell him to *hurry*," she said more loudly, hoping the driver would hear. "Tell him it's very important."

The driver did hear, and his answer was

to jam on the brakes, pull into the kerb and switch off the engine.

"Just you try hurrying," he barked, "with a blockage in the carburettor! I've had this lark before."

"Well — can't you fix it?" cried Terry. "We've got to get a move on."

"I'm a taxi driver not a bloody mechanic, mate."

"I'll do it," said Terry, opening the car door. "It shouldn't take a minute — it's my job."

The man turned round in his seat and glared at Terry, his eyebrows twitching. "Not bloody likely, you're not," he snapped. "I'm not having no young kids monkeying about with my engine!"

Veronica groaned. She expected Terry to lose his temper as well, but he just said in a calm friendly voice, "I know how you feel, but I've worked at Parker's Garage for three years and I'm pretty sure I could fix it for you, if you wouldn't mind me having a look."

The man sniffed and shrugged and lit a cigarette. "O.K., mate. See what you can do. Only it's strictly off the record — and if you do any damage you'll pay for it, get that straight."

"Yes, of course," said Terry, and in a flash he was out of the car and opening up the bonnet, his long hair gleaming gold under a near-by street lamp.

Veronica was overwhelmed with love and gratitude. Once again he had proved the value of "bending like the willow." And yet there were plenty of people who would say he was being weak and wishy-washy and ought to "give as good as he got."

She patted her father's arm. "It'll be O.K., Dad," she said. "I'm sure he'll fix it quickly. He's a super mechanic." She looked at her watch again. "It's three minutes to, but surely Mother wouldn't *really* do anything — would she?"

"I don't know," he said, watching anxiously as Terry worked under the bonnet with a little adjustable spanner he had in his pocket. "I just don't know. . . ."

Terry was holding some kind of small bolt up to the street lamp and peering at it with one eye shut. Then he put it to his lips and blew into it several times. He squinted at it again and after a few moments gave them the thumbs-up sign.

"Easy when you know how," he said as he sat down again beside Veronica, wiping his hands on his handkerchief. "Away we go, then."

The driver threw his cigarette, still alight,

out of the window. "Thanks, mate," he grunted as he started the engine. "Sorry, but I couldn't risk my cab, could I? How was I to know you worked at Parker's?"

"Course not. That's O.K. You'll step on it, won't you? We're supposed to be there by nine."

The man looked at his watch. "Bit tight for nine. Five or ten past, maybe, if the lights are right."

Mr ⸺ gave a lown groan. "Your mother said nine," he told Veronica in an undertone. " 'Straight up nine,' she said, 'or you'll be sorry'. . . ."

"P'raps it was just a threat," whispered Veronica, but she was trembling with anxiety. Her father had laboured over those model ships for years. Ever since she could remember, he had spent his leisure time in that little shed, carving away with loving care, perfecting every tiny part. Veronica often used to sit in there with him. When she was a little girl she would play with her dolls, or watch entranced as the galleons took shape. Later she would sit on his bench and read or do her homework. Nobody knew, as she did, just how passionately he loved those ships.

The lights *were* against them and it was after ten past nine when at last the taxi drew up outside Number 5, Moon Street. Terry told Mr. Mason to go straight into the house with Veronica while he paid the taxi and looked after the suitcase.

She followed her father as he ran to the front door and she had never felt more frightened in her life.

1?

he lights were on in the hall.

"Ethel — we're here!" shouted Mr. Mason. Ethel — Veronica's come back — she's here!"

There was no reply; the house seemed deserted. He burst into the kitchen, where the lights were also on, and went racing through the back door into the yard.

Veronica hardly dared to follow him; she stood in the kitchen doorway as he ran across to his workshop and switched on the light.

"They're all *right!*" he cried. "My ships are all right!" He was inside the shed, searching the shelves for signs of damage.

Veronica stood in the yard and tears of relief came flooding to her eyes as she saw him handling one of his galleons with trembling tenderness, as a child might caress a beloved doll which has been in danger of destruction.

After a minute he came out and took Veronica by the arm. "She didn't mean it, after all," he said, and there were tears on his own cheeks, too; she could see them glittering in the light from the kitchen window. "Thank God — she didn't mean it!"

"Where is she, then?" said Veronica. "If she wanted me back so much, why isn't she here to see me?"

"I don't know — she can't be far — she'd never leave the lights on. I hope she's all right — she was in an awful state when I left."

They went into the house and Mr. Mason called again: "Ethel — where are you? Veronica's here!"

There was no reply, no sound but the familiar noises of the street — the baby crying at Number 7, somebody's television blaring through an open window, the drone of an aircraft.

Mr. Mason pulled at his tie. "I'll just go upstairs and see if she's in the bathroom," he said. "She can't have gone far, anyway — she never leaves the lights on."

"I'll go and tell Terry that everything's

O.K.," said Veronica. "He won't like to come in after the way she treated him on Saturday."

Mr. Mason was halfway up the stairs and he turned and smiled down at her. "He's a wonderful lad," he said. "You couldn't have anyone better. Take him to the workshop and show him my ships — tell him he can have one if he likes. Just let him take whichever one he fancies."

"Oh *thanks*, Dad. He'll be thrilled."

The front door was open and she saw that Terry was sitting on her case, looking up at the full moon which had just emerged from behind a bank of cloud.

She went out and joined him. "Terry, the ships are O.K.," she cried. "Mother isn't here — we can't think what's happened because she never goes out and leaves the lights on. Dad's just gone to see if she's upstairs."

Terry said, "Thank God there's no damage done. D'you think I ought to go away? If your mother sees me it won't help matters, will it?"

"No — don't go! Please! Dad says you can have one of his galleons — whichever you like. Come through to the shed and choose one."

"Honest?"

"Yeah. He thinks you're great." She looked at him fondly. "You were marvellous with that taxi man — the old devil!"

"He wasn't so bad, really, you know. He wouldn't accept any fare."

"It was only because you handled him right."

Terry grinned. "Most folks are O.K. if you handle 'em right."

"Give way a little — like your song."

"Yeah."

They went into the house, and Terry put the case in the hall. Veronica looked anxiously up the stairs. "Dad," she called uneasily, "is she there?"

He appeared on the landing. "No — not a sign. I can't think where she's got to. I'll go over and see if she's at Mrs. Wainwright's."

"Yeah. I'll show Terry the workshop."

"Thanks for the ship, Mr. Mason," said Terry. "I'll really treasure it."

"Wait till you've seen it before you say that, Terry."

"I don't need to. Ronny's told me how beautiful they are."

Veronica was so happy to be showing Terry the workshop that for the moment she forgot her apprehensions about her mother. She took him through the kitchen and out into the yard, running ahead to switch on the workshop light.

"Come on," she said. "You'll love it in here.

You'll want to start making galleons yourself."

As she went through the door of the shed a train went by, rattling the tools on her father's bench, and she was suddenly seized by a sickening terror. The railway line! Supposing her mother had become so demented when her father didn't return by nine that she wanted to destroy herself instead of the ships. . . .

Her heart began to thump and she turned to Terry, gripping his arm and staring wildly into his bewildered face. "Terry — the railway! Supposing Mother's done it after all!"

"You think it's really possible?"

She nodded.

"You stay here," said Terry. "Stay with your father. I'll go and see if I can find out anything."

" Oh, Terry — "

He hugged her for a second and ran out through the back gate towards the railway track.

19

Veronica ran into the house and met her father in the hall.

"She's not there," he gasped. "There's no one in at Mrs. Wainwright's."

"Oh, Dad — I'm so frightened! The railway line — could she have — you know? Terry's gone to look."

"I don't think she'd do that," he said, but his voice was shaking and the familiar red patches were staining the sides of his jaws.

"Come out the back way," cried Veronica, dragging him by the hand. "Quick — I want to look for Terry."

They hurried across the yard and out onto the path that skirted the railway. There was a low wall dividing it from the bank of grass and weeds that sloped down to the track. Veronica peered over the wall, searching for a glimpse of Terry, but the moon had vanished behind the clouds and she could see nothing but a trench of darkness between herself and the lighted windows of the houses at the other side of the railway lines.

She leaned over the wall with her father, straining her eyes in both directions, but it was too dark to see anything. Her father held her arm very tightly, but he did not speak. She could feel him trembling and she knew he was overcome with anxiety.

Suddenly the moon came riding out from behind a cloud and the scene was transformed; the rails shone like quicksilver and you could see every detail of a rubbish tip on the opposite slope, the rusting tins half overgrown with grass. But there was no one in sight except the signalman in his little lighted box a hundred yards or so across the track to the left. The rails curved away behind the box and were lost to view. Maybe Terry was just out of sight round the corner. Veronica could see the signalman at work, walking about in the box like a tiny puppet, and after a while he began pulling at the big levers. She heard the signals clatter and saw them flash in the moonlight, realising with a new pang of dread, that another train was due.

She clutched at her father's hand but she dared not say what was in her mind. She could only lean farther over the wall, straining her eyes for Terry, praying that her mother was somewhere safe and cosy, chattering about her Church Bazaar or even raging to some neighbour about her daughter's behaviour. That wouldn't matter, so long as she was safe. She could say what she liked. . . .

"I expect she's just gone to see someone — collecting for the Bazaar or something," said Veronica. "I expect she forgot the lights because — because she was sort of funny, like you said."

Her father squeezed her hand but he did not reply. The moon had vanished again, leaving the track in semidarkness. The signal box and the lighted windows of the houses seemed twice as bright without the moonlight.

"I'm going to look for Terry," cried Veronica at last. "I can't stay here — I can't ——"

Her father held her firmly. "No, pet — you mustn't go down there — there's a train due any minute. Terry'll be back soon — I'm sure he will."

Veronica tried to free herself from her father's grip. "I want Terry — let me go!" She felt as if she was losing control; she had to move, she had to do *something*. . . .

"Stay with me just now, Veronica. I need you."

Those were the words that calmed her: "I need you." She realised that he needed her comfort — perhaps even more than she needed his.

"I must call to him, then," she said. "He might be lost down there. He might not know now to get back to us."

"All right. We'll both shout. Take a deep breath — one, two, three — *Terry! Terry!*"

Together they yelled as loudly as they could, but there was no reply and Veronica was sure she could hear the distant rumble of the approaching train.

"*Terry!*"

Still there was silence except for the faint vibration of the train and the wailing of the baby at Number 7. Suddenly Mr. Mason cried out, "I'm going next door — I'm going to see if they know anything. Come with me, won't you?"

"No — no, Dad, please. I must stay and watch out for Terry."

"All right — I won't be long." And he vanished into the gloom.

The moon came out again a moment later, brilliantly clear of the clouds, and it was then that Veronica caught sight of someone walking on the railway track. It was a tall stumbling figure and in the bright moonlight Veronica could see quite clearly that it was her mother.

"*Dad!*" she shrieked. "*Dad!*" She tried to call again but no sound would come. Her limbs seemed paralysed and all she could do was to stare in speechless terror as her mother wandered slowly between the shining rails and the rumble of the train grew louder every second.

Mrs. Mason was ambling along the railway track in a vague, leisurely manner, as if she was out for a stroll in the fields and Veronica wanted to shriek at her to com off the lines, she wanted to climb the wall and race down the slope to drag her away, but e was quite unable to move or to utter a so nd. It was like a nightmare; she was helpless, ozen with terror.

She could hear the train approaching and she was almost fainting with dread, when she caught sight of Terry. He was just coming into view round the curve of the track beyond the signal box, his hair bright in the moon— light. He could not have seen Mrs. Mason because he was walking quite slowly, and sud— denly Veronica found her voice.

"*Terry!*" she screamed. "*Quick* — she there — on the *line!*"

He paused for an instant and then she saw him racing towards her mother at a fantastic speed, hair flying, arms pumping like pistons. It was like a scene in one of those melodramatic old films — the train approaching, the last moment rescue; only it was not a beautiful girl on the line but a middle-aged woman, demented with grief and guilt. . . .

The roar of the train was now so loud that Veronica hardly dared to watch in case the two of them should be mown down together. Terry was on the track himself, right in the path of the train which was already in sight, its lighted carriages swinging round the curve. He came up behind Mrs. Mason, seized her in his arms and half carried, half dragged her off the track. A few moments later, the train went thundering by, its passengers sitting calmly in their seats, dozing or reading papers, quite oblivious of the tragedy which had only just been averted.

Sick and shaking, Veronica leaned on the wall, while Terry hoisted her mother across his back as firemen do. She did not seem to be offering any resistance, but leaned on him limply with her limbs as loose as a rag doll. Slowly and with small, careful steps, Terry began to carry her up the grassy slope towards the house. It was obviously a very difficult task and he kept stopping to secure his footing.

"Terry — can you manage?" cried Veronica, as he came staggering towards her.

He paused for breath and gasped out, "Get the ambulance — phone for the ambulance ——"

She hesitated for a moment because she didn't really know how to go about it, but this was no time for questions and she rushed away down the path towards the main road where there was a telephone box.

In the box she was almost too distraught to read the instructions properly but at last she was through to the ambulance department, giving the address and trying to answer their questions sensibly.

When she got back to the house Terry and her father were carrying Mrs. Mason into the kitchen. Her eyes were closed and her face was a yellowish grey. Her hair, usually so sleekly combed, was wild and untidy, with loose strands hanging across her eyes. Terry's face was running with sweat, and his blue anorak had damp stains under the armpits.

"The ambulance is coming," gasped Veronica.

Terry muttered, "Good girl." He was carrying her mother through the kitchen to the sitting room, with Mr. Mason holding the door open and murmuring, "Soon be all right . . . soon be all right . . ." in a valiant effort to comfort everybody.

Mrs. Mason's eyes were open now, but she seemed hardly aware of her surroundings and when they laid her on the sofa she closed her eyes again and made no movement except to moan from time to time and to take deep shuddering breaths. Veronica guessed that she was very ill and she longed for the ambulance to come so that she could have the proper treatment.

"Ethel?" whispered Mr. Mason. "You're going to be all right — we're looking after you ——"

Her eyes fluttered open and she looked at him blankly and then at Veronica, but there was no sign of recognition; even when she saw Terry, who was sitting on a chair beside the television set, she registered no emotion.

"She's miles away," whispered Mr. Mason. "I wish to God the ambulance would come — I just don't know how to cope with this."

At that moment Veronica saw the ambulance drive past the window.

"There it is!" she cried.

Terry jumped up. "I'll go," he said. "I expect they'll bring a stretcher."

Before long Mrs. Mason was in the ambulance and Mr. Mason came into the sitting room, hunching himself into his overcoat.

"I'll go with her, of course," he said to Veronica who was standing by the window with Terry. "They're sure to keep her in for quite a while. You'd better go back with Terry, hadn't you?"

Veronica nodded. She was too exhausted to speak, but she felt the stirring of happiness under all the torment.

Terry said, "I'll look after her — don't worry."

"I know you will. And — Terry — I've got no words to — to thank you for what you did. I'll never be able to — "

"Don't try," said Terry. "Thank God I made it in time."

Veronica managed to say, "Daddy — will she be all right?"

"I'm sure she will. It'll take time, but they can work miracles these days."

"I'll try and help — all I can," said Veronica. "I know I've done things — the wrong way."

"So have I," said her father. "So have I."

An ambulance man put his head round the door. "Ready, sir?"

"Bye, Daddy," said Veronica. "Phone me at Terry's and — "

"I will." He stumbled across the room and embraced her for a moment. Then he reached out for Terry's hand. "Be happy, you two. You deserve everything."

They watched the ambulance drive away and Terry slumped onto the sofa and pulled

Veronica down beside him. "My poor chick," he said. "You must be all in."

She took a deep breath and summoned all the best that was in her. "No, I'm not," she told him. "I can't wait to get back and finish peeling those potatoes."